# Her Father's Choice

# Her Father's Choice

## A Pride and Prejudice Variation

### LEENIE BROWN

LEENIE B BOOKS
HALIFAX

Cover design by Leenie B Books. Images sourced from Deposit Photos and Period Images.

ISBNs: 978-1-989410-94-3 (ebook); 978-1-989410-95-0 (print); 978-1-989410-96-7 (large print)

# Contents

*Dedication*

To my friend, Zoe
Thank you for your encouragement and
patience and for believing I could finish that chap-
ter or fix that issue when I was not certain I could.

# Prologue

*Not handsome enough but with fine eyes?* Mr. Bennet chuckled to himself as he tucked himself away in the corner of the drawing room at Lucas Lodge. From here he could keep an eye on his daughters and listen to various conversations as people moved from place to place. Most of them would, at one point or another, pass through the door near him to the room beyond where there was a table laid out with various forms of refreshment.

He chuckled again as he repeated Mr. Darcy's comment to Miss Bingley to himself. Fine eyes, indeed! His Lizzy possessed the most expressive eyes of any lady Mr. Bennet had ever met. One look let you know quite clearly what she was thinking.

"Fine eyes," he muttered. It was as he had suspected when he had first met Mr. Darcy — Elizabeth

*1*

would make him a fine wife. It had not taken long for that reserved and well-educated gentleman to fall under the spell of a lady whose mind was just as astute as his own. Not handsome enough? The man must have been in some foul mood to have spoken so harshly and, he added with some force to himself, wrongly. Elizabeth was not Jane, but she was by no means lacking in beauty.

But that was the fly in the ointment. Elizabeth had heard the slight Mr. Darcy had made at the assembly and taken such a strong disliking to the man. Mr. Bennet sighed and shook his head. He knew that bringing the two together would be quite the undertaking — excessively difficult but utterly necessary if he wished to see Elizabeth well-matched and happy. Mr. Darcy was, in every way that Mr. Bennet could determine, the gentleman who was his daughter's equal.

"I tried to arrange a dance between them," said Sir William as he handed his long-time friend a glass of lemonade. "But, she is quite set against him, it seems."

"I saw," Mr. Bennet replied. "And then I heard him mention her fine eyes."

"Indeed?"

Bennet nodded. "Miss Bingley is quite put out by the comment. I do not envy his position of having an unhappy woman yapping at his elbow." He raised his eyebrows and smirked as he took a sip of his drink.

Sir William lifted his glass in salute. "Hear, hear. I have had it happen a time or two in the past eight and twenty years myself. There is nothing quite like the continual complaining of a disgruntled woman robed in supposed humour to try one's nerves."

"He is a patient one. I am sure I could not abide Miss Bingley's comments so graciously as he." Mr. Bennet shifted in his chair. "It is a good sign, for if he can tolerate Miss Bingley in a fit of pique, he should be able to handle my Lizzy."

"Aye, he should, but Lizzy's tongue and mind are a bit sharper. And her opinions are not so easily swayed." There was a hint of caution in Sir William's voice.

Mr. Bennet knew that his friend agreed with him about Mr. Darcy and Elizabeth making a fine match. That had not, however, stopped Sir William from voicing his concern, repeatedly, that

Elizabeth could not be swayed from her current dislike of the gentleman.

"She will come around, although," Mr. Bennet drew out the word and lowered his voice, "that may not happen until after they are married."

Sir William laughed. "Exactly how do you propose we get her to marry him when she does not like him? Surely, you would not suggest a compromise?"

Mr. Bennet tapped his finger against the side of his glass. "I would do almost anything to assure the happiness of my Lizzy, even if it meant bearing her anger and forcing her hand."

He watched Elizabeth, who was talking intently to her dear friend, Charlotte Lucas. He smiled as she sneaked a third glance at Mr. Darcy. If Mr. Bennet was not mistaken, and he rarely was when it came to understanding Elizabeth, she was fascinated by the man from Derbyshire. It was a fascination that he was certain was foreign to her.

"I pray it does not come to it, but if a compromise is necessary, can I count on your assistance?"

Sir William studied his friend and then Elizabeth for a moment. "You are convinced she will be happy?"

"Completely."

Sir William sighed. It was a sound of resignation and the same one he always made when he was about to bow to Mr. Bennet's wishes.

"Then, my friend," he said, "I will happily assist you with whatever you need."

# Chapter 1

November 26, 1811

The music swirled about Elizabeth as she completed the final few steps of the dance. As the last notes of the song faded into the expanse of Netherfield's ballroom, she dipped a curtsey and moved silently away from her dancing partner. The swirling feeling, however, did not die with the music.

From the corner of her eye, she could see Miss Bingley moving toward her. Speaking to anyone, let alone Miss Bingley, was not something she wished to do at present, so seeing an opportunity to slip away from the crowds, she took it. She smiled at her father as she slid behind him and out of the room into the hallway.

Assuring herself that no one had seen her escape, she hurried to the library. A need for solitude and a place to gather her thoughts and sort through the strange feelings that had her nerves all aflutter consumed her. Quietly, she clicked the door shut behind her and retrieved a book of poetry from the shelf. It was one of the books she had enjoyed reading when she had stayed here to tend to her sister.

~*~

Darcy watched Miss Elizabeth slip off her shoes and tuck her small feet under her skirts as she curled into her chair and flipped the pages of her book. His own book lay open on his lap, but not one word had entered his mind for it was filled with the lady who now presented such a charming picture before him.

*This*, he thought to himself, *this is how an evening at home should be spent.* The thought both shocked and pleased him. He shook his head and smiled, for he could not help it even in his unsettled state of mind. Thoughts of Miss Elizabeth often led him to smile. He allowed himself several moments to consider her and play again in his mind many of their interactions before he turned his mind to his book.

*As fair as thou, my bonnie lass,*
*So deep in* luve *am I;*

*And I will love thee still, my dear,*
*Till a' the seas gang dry.*[1]

Darcy closed the book. *So deep in love am I.* The words of Mr. Burns' poem repeated themselves in his mind. He tipped his head to the right as he once again studied his reading companion and the truth of those words from the poem repeated themselves once again in his mind. *So deep in love am I.* That must be what ailed him. His disquiet, his agitation of spirit, his joy in having her near, and his torment when hearing her speak of another were not symptoms that his heart *might be* in danger of being engaged, as he had thought, but rather they were signs that it was already engaged and, he feared, to an unalterable extent.

Softly, he lay his book on the table next to his chair and rose to leave. He would return later to retrieve the book so that he might ponder the words and what he was to do about his heart.

~*~

1. *Burns, Robert, and Anonymous. "A DAY WITH THE POET BURNS." The Project Gutenberg EBook of A Day with the Poet Burns by Anonymous. Project Gutenberg, 15 Feb. 2011. Web. Poem quoted is "My Luve is Like a Red, Red Rose." Book originally published by Hodder and Stoughton, London.*

Elizabeth glanced up at Darcy as he walked to the door and flipped yet another unread page. The book had not been able to capture her mind or quiet her spirit. The room still spun slowly, her heart still fluttered, and her eyes were drawn of their own accord to the man sitting across the room from her. Perhaps once he took his leave of the room, she would be able to find the peace she sought.

She turned her mind back to her book; but it was of no use, the desire to read seemed to be leaving with Mr. Darcy. So, she stood, smoothed her skirts, and slipped her feet into her slippers.

The door opened as Darcy reached it, and Elizabeth's aunt, Mrs. Philips, entered. She looked from Mr. Darcy to Elizabeth, who was still smoothing her skirts, and then peered around the room as if searching for someone or something. Her eyes grew wide, and her hand flew to her chest.

"Oh," she said. "Oh, my. Oh, Lizzy. And...and Mr. Darcy." She spun on her heels and very nearly ran from the room. "Mr. Bennet," she called. "Mr. Bennet, you are needed."

The horror of what her aunt must think washed over Elizabeth. "I must stop her," she said as she moved toward the door, but Darcy stopped her. She looked first at the hand which lay on her arm and then to the face of the owner of that hand.

"The damage has already been done," he said softly. "If you follow after her, she will only make a greater spectacle when she either scolds or questions you. It is best to await your father here." He led her back to her chair. Reluctantly, it seemed, he let go of her arm as she took a seat. "Are you well?" he asked.

"I hardly know," she replied. Thoughts of the things her aunt might be saying filled her mind. She sought a solution, an explanation that might explain her current circumstances in such a way as to repair her reputation. She knew that once her aunt spun the tale to one and all about the few seconds of what she had seen in the library, her reputation would be well and truly tarnished. Aunt Philips was the worst gossip.

She watched Mr. Darcy pace around the room and replied to his inquiries after her health each time he asked if she was well. He sat for a moment but stood again and resumed his pacing, which only stopped when her father entered. Then she noted how very rigid his stance became. She could only imagine he was just as unhappy about their current situation as she was.

"Papa," she said rising and going to him, "it is not how my aunt presented it."

Her father pulled her into his embrace.

"I have no doubt of that, but it is not about what has happened. It is about what others think has happened." He spoke gently to her as if attempting to keep the horrible reality of the situation in which she found herself from causing her too much pain. "I do not doubt your honour, but you know how the gossips work."

~*~

He released her from his arms and grasping her chin, forced her to look at him. The anguish in her eyes was nearly his undoing. "Have a seat while we discuss what can be done to save your reputation," he faltered for a moment before adding what he knew would play most heavily upon her heart, "and the reputation of our family." He clenched his jaw as he saw her eyes grow wide and fill with tears. This needed to be done. She would be happy eventually.

"There is only one option, sir." Mr. Darcy pulled Mr. Bennet's attention away from Elizabeth.

"I must marry your daughter. My reputation may be tainted slightly by a situation such as this, but the damage that would be done to Miss Elizabeth...."

He let his thought fade away and stood there, silently, waiting as Mr. Bennet gave him a sweeping glance from head to foot and back again. It was good to see he had not overestimated Mr. Darcy's honour. That would make things somewhat easier.

"I believe you have the right of it, Mr. Darcy. There seem to be few other options. I know my wife's sister is not one to keep a story such as this to herself. I fear the entirety of Mr. Bingley's guests has already come to know about this *supposed* compromise." He emphasized the word supposed to let both Elizabeth and Mr. Darcy know that he did not believe a compromise had actually taken place.

"No, Papa, please," she begged him. He could see the panic that gripped Elizabeth for it was etched in her expression, and it tore at his heart.

"Elizabeth, there is no other option. You will marry Mr. Darcy." His voice was gentle but firm, and he used her full name instead of Lizzy so that she would know there was no hope of his changing his mind.

"No," she said softly as she buried her face in her hands and allowed the tears she had been fighting to fall.

He put his arm around her shoulder and pulled her close and placed a kiss on her hair. "My dear daughter, it is for the best. Aunt Philips is not known for her discretion, and the story of your being alone in the library with Mr. Darcy will be circulated, and embellishments will be added. Your betrothal is all that will save your reputation. We must also think of your sisters."

Her shoulders shook as she sobbed quietly, but she nodded her head as if she understood the reality of the situation.

Mr. Bennet swallowed the lump in his throat and strengthened his resolve as he reminded himself that this was for the best, even if his heart broke at seeing her so unhappy.

"It will be a good thing, Lizzy. I know you do not see it now, but I truly believe there is no one better suited to you than Mr. Darcy." He a second kiss on the top of her head. "Dry your eyes." He gave her hand a squeeze as he stood to address Mr. Darcy. "I do not question your honour. I am convinced this is nothing more than an unfortunate chain of

events, but the gossip will not present it as such."
His conscience pricked him as he said it. Truly, it
was not Darcy's honour he questioned as much as
his own.

"How shall we proceed?" Darcy's voice was
tight.

"It might be best if we give everyone time to
adjust to the sudden circumstances," suggested Sir
William, who had only moments ago, joined them
in the library. "A meeting could be arranged for
tomorrow."

"That is an excellent idea, I should think," Mr.
Bennet agreed. A few hours to accept the reality
of what was their future would make any further
discussions less fraught with emotions – or so he
hoped. "Do you agree, Mr. Darcy?"

Darcy nodded his acceptance before asking,
"May I have a few moments with Miss Elizabeth
before she leaves?"

Mr. Bennet gave him a sympathetic smile, "I
think that is acceptable to allow."

The request, coupled with the look of concern
on Darcy's face, eased his mind a bit. His daughter
would be loved. Indeed, it appeared she already

was. If only she could see past her first impression of the gentleman.

Mr. Bennet had attempted to paint Darcy in a favourable light, but no matter how hard he had tried, Elizabeth had clung to her opinion that Darcy was proud and disdained everything about her, her family, and the neighbourhood. She was wrong, of course. He had done some shooting with Darcy and Bingley and had found both gentlemen to be pleasant; although, Darcy was more reserved and thoughtful.

He pulled the door closed as he and Sir William entered the hall.

"We have done what is best, have we not?" Mr. Bennet looked to his friend for reassurance.

Sir William shrugged. "Whether it is best or not, it is done. We must trust that they will eventually be happy together." He leaned against the door frame across from Mr. Bennet. "Consider the facts. Collins was set to make an offer which would have led to a great upheaval in your household when Elizabeth refused him — for you know she would."

Mr. Bennet nodded his agreement. Elizabeth had made her dislike for the gentleman perfectly clear to everyone save to her mother and Mr. Collins.

Sir William continued, "Then, there were Miss Bingley's comments about quitting the neighbourhood. That will not happen so quickly now, which will give Jane a greater chance of being happily matched. After all, news of one wedding often leads to news of others. And," he held up his finger to highlight the point, "it would be desirable to Bingley to be closely related to Darcy. His standing would increase and the felicity between their wives would serve both men well." He shifted and crossed one leg over the other. "There is also the fact that Mr. Wickham has been showing particular attention to Elizabeth, and from rumors I have heard, he is not the sort of man a father wishes to have pay court to his daughter." He sighed. "There are no guarantees, but I do believe your choice will prove to be best...in time."

Mr. Bennet leaned his head back and closed his eyes. He prayed that he had made the right choice and that, one day, his daughter and his new son would forgive him for his interference.

# Chapter 2

Within the library, Darcy cautiously took a seat next to Miss Elizabeth. He longed to pull her to his chest and assure her all would be well, but he could not. Instead, he placed his handkerchief in her lap, giving her the only token of his care that he was allowed.

She took the piece of cloth and dried her eyes as she mumbled her thanks. Then with a slight shake of her head to gain control of her emotions, she spoke. "I am so very sorry. I should not have come in here. But the people and the noise and the..." Her control failed, and she slipped back into tears.

"It was overwhelming." Darcy grasped his knee so that he would not take her hand. Those were the very reasons he had sought refuge in the library. Those and the wish to contemplate the desire to relieve Wickham of his life which had overtaken him during his and Miss Elizabeth's dance. It was a desire he had felt once before but never with such intensity as when he considered Elizabeth being taken in by the wastrel.

She nodded. "And now you are tied to me because I allowed my desire for solace to over-whelm my good sense." She buried her face in his handkerchief. "I am so very sorry, but my fam-ily...my sisters..." The words were muffled some-what by the cloth she held to her face.

"No, I should have made my presence known or left as soon as you entered, but I chose to stay." Colour crept up his neck. He prayed she would not ask him why he had made that choice.

She shook her head. "I knew you were there. I chose to ignore propriety. Oh, what you must think of me!" Though she had uncovered her face, her eyes were still firmly focused on the handker-chief which she wound in her hands.

"And what *you* must think of *me*." He gave her a gentle smile as she peeked up at him. "We both chose to ignore propriety."

She nodded.

"But, what concerns me more is that you find the prospect of marriage to me to be so horrible as to bring you to tears. Surely, I cannot be that bad." There was a hint of uncertainty in his voice which made the statement sound more like a question than a statement.

Elizabeth looked at her hands again. How did one tell the man you were to marry that although he stirred deep and strong emotion in you, you were not sure if you even liked him? "It is the shock of the situation, I am sure," she mumbled.

"Of course," he agreed, although she suspected he did not. They passed a very long and strained moment in silence. "You have not yet deciphered my character. You do not trust me." There was that uncertainty in his voice again though it sounded more pained than questioning this time.

"I can neither trust nor distrust you, sir," she said. For some reason, she felt a need to ease his discomfort.

"We do not need to marry immediately. How long would you like for our betrothal to be?"

She shrugged, but her mind whirled. Her mother would be unbearable and the whispering in Meryton would follow her wherever she went. While the thought of marrying a man she barely knew frightened her more than she was willing to admit even to herself, she knew that remaining in Meryton and at Longbourn would be just as unbearable.

"There are at least three readings. I see no reason to delay it beyond that. I know you are anxious to quit the neighbourhood."

"I admit that I would prefer to be in more familiar and comfortable surroundings, but I am more concerned that you be at ease."

She peeked at him once again, her brows furrowed as they had during their dance when she questioned him. He smiled. "I can see you are once again trying to read my character. I promise to answer any questions you may have, but there will be no reading of the banns. We will marry by special license."

Her eyes widened. "Why?"

"My aunt." He gave her a wry smile. "Mr. Collins' patroness," he rolled his eyes, and she caught a laugh just before it burst forth, "Lady Catherine de Bourgh is, as I am sure your cousin has made you aware, my aunt."

"And this demands a special license?" The handkerchief lay knotted but still on her lap.

"She expects me to marry her daughter. I have

never had any intention of marrying my cousin, and I am not, as I am sure has been said, betrothed to her. There is no arrangement, but that does not mean my aunt will not be greatly displeased. I do not wish to give her the opportunity to cause an issue by making a statement in reply to the banns."

"You are not betrothed?"

He shook his head. "No. It is a great desire of my aunt's, but it is not mine." He sighed. "I do not like family discord. It is why I have not been more forceful in making my position known. Indeed, it is why I do not complain more frequently to Bingley regarding his sisters. I consider him as a brother. He is not family by blood, but he is family by extension."

There was a soft knock at the door.

"Our time is up, Miss Elizabeth. May I call on you when I come to Longbourn to meet with your father? Perhaps, if Bingley accompanies me, he and I could join you and your sister on a walk, and you may begin to question me." His mouth tipped up only on one side, giving him a rather playful look that startled Elizabeth in a most pleasant way.

"I would like that," she said, and she was surprised to realize just how much she actually meant it.

Mr. Bennet opened the door just as Elizabeth smiled at Mr. Darcy when he stood to leave.

"You are well?" Her father asked hopefully as he looked from her to Mr. Darcy.

"I am resigned," she said. "I know that I cannot put my wishes before my duty to my sisters. Perhaps it is as you said and will be for the best." She hugged his arm as they walked toward the door of the library. "He was exceedingly kind just now. Not at all proud."

Darcy paused in the hall as her words reached him. He hastened his steps and sought Bingley, who was just wishing Miss Bennet a good night. "I must speak with you," he said softly as he stood near his friend.

"Oh, Mr. Darcy!" Mrs. Bennet's shrill voice caused him to grimace slightly. "You are a sly one. Pretending to not like Lizzy and then proposing. It is quite surprising, I assure you. We were positively certain you disapproved of her, and I would not blame you if you did. She can be quite the outspoken sort, and her beauty is nothing compared to Jane."

Jane flinched at the comment and extended her hand to Mr. Darcy as if wishing him a good night. "I must apologize for my mother. I believe she has had a bit too much punch." She smiled that serene smile of hers, and Darcy wondered for the first time how much she might conceal behind her facade.

Gently, she guided her mother and younger sisters out the door with a quick look over her shoulder toward where Elizabeth walked with her father.

Darcy shook his head. Miss Bennet was removing her mother before a greater scene ensued. He had obviously misjudged her depths, and if he had been wrong in this, perhaps he was wrong in not perceiving her affection for Bingley.

"I will wait for you in the library."

Bingley shot him an amused look. "Have you not spent enough time in there yet tonight?"

Darcy scowled. He was in no mood for Bingley's teasing at present. The words he had just heard from Elizabeth were still stinging far too much for him to be pleasant.

"I will be there directly," Bingley said with a nod before turning to Mr. Bennet.

~*~

Darcy paced the library as he waited for Bingley.

He mulled Elizabeth's words over in his mind. *Not at all proud and exceedingly kind.* She had seemed surprised to find him so.

"Am I proud?" he blurted as Bingley entered the room.

"Not improperly so." Bingley removed his jacket and unbuttoned his waistcoat before lowering himself into a chair with a sigh. "Of course, people have to get to know you before they realize it."

"What do you mean?" Darcy stopped in front of Bingley's chair and looked down at him.

"Your serious expression and reserve can be misunderstood as being aloof and disdainful."

Darcy pondered that for a moment. He could see how that could be. Not that being able to agree with a negative description of oneself made the description any more enjoyable to hear.

"Did you think I did not approve of Miss Elizabeth?"

Bingley laughed. "You did tell me she was not handsome enough to tempt you, a fact that, Miss Bennet assures me, her sister knows."

"I may have been wrong about her."

Bingley laughed again. "Well, I should hope so.

One does not wish to find himself married to a lady who is merely tolerable and not tempting."

"No," said Darcy, shaking his head. "Miss Bennet. She quite possibly likes you." He sat in a chair and leaned his head back looking up at the ceiling. "I was wrong about Miss Elizabeth as well. She is quite handsome." He scrubbed his face. "However, she finds me proud and was surprised that I could be kind."

"That does not bode well for a marriage," said Bingley, studying his friend. It was rare to see Darcy so distraught. "So, there was no secret assignation as implied?"

Darcy groaned. "No. I read a book, and Miss Elizabeth read a book. I sat here, and she was across the room. There was nothing worthy of scandal that happened in here tonight."

"But her aunt saw you together."

"I was just leaving the room when Mrs. Philips came in in search of Miss Elizabeth. She pushed past me into the room and saw Miss Elizabeth putting on her slippers and smoothing her skirt...as any lady would do after sitting for an extended period of time." He sighed. "Before I could stop her, she was off calling for Mr. Bennet, as I am sure you and all your guests heard." He rested an arm across his eyes. "A brief discussion followed between myself and Mr. Bennet and then between Mr. Bennet and Miss Elizabeth." He drew a deep breath. "She wept at the thought of marrying me, Bingley. She wept."

Bingley could feel the pain in his friend's voice. "Do you love her?"

"I did not realize it until this evening, but yes, I believe I do love her."

"Then show her the man who is my friend. If you displayed him more often, I would not be able to claim so many angels, for they would be tripping over their slippers to be with you."

Darcy laughed lightly. Bingley always knew how best to distill a complex situation down to something dashed simple. "Are you saying you find me irresistible, Bingley?"

Bingley laughed loudly. "No! No! I am merely suggesting you could be irresistible to women if you would show your true self to them." He continued laughing. "Of course, you really only need one lady to find you irresistible."

"Yes, one lady who *must* marry me, but presently, I fear, does not even like me very much."

Bingley rose. "You need sleep; though, I doubt you will get much."

Darcy stood with him. "I believe you are right." He followed Bingley to the door. "I am to meet tomorrow afternoon with Mr. Bennet to discuss particulars of the marriage agreement. I have asked Miss Elizabeth to take a walk with me, and she has consented. I told her I would bring you with me so that you could keep Miss Bennet company."

Bingley turned to look at Darcy. "You agree Miss Bennet likes me?"

"I believe you could be right, but my opinion on matters feminine seems to be sadly lacking, so I would put more confidence in your own feelings than in mine."

"But you believe it is possible?"

"Yes, Bingley, I do."

"So," Bingley said as they entered the hall, "I was right, and you, the great counselor and guide, were wrong?"

"Bingley," Darcy growled, "have a care. I have had a rather trying night."

"Not as trying as mine is about to be," Bingley said as he saw his sister Caroline approaching.

"Good night. You will understand if I leave you

now," Darcy said as he nodded to Caroline and took the stairs to his room two at a time before either Bingley could say anything to him.

# Chapter 3

Elizabeth blew out a breath in an attempt to calm her nerves as she fastened her pelisse. There was no reason for her to be nervous about talking to Mr. Darcy. She had spoken to him on many occasions and never once had felt even the slightest amount of trepidation, but today, she was struggling to keep her nerves from running away with her sense. Last night, she had resolved, after a lengthy sisterly chat and many tears, that she would accept her fate with as much alacrity as she could contrive. However, making a decision was proving easier than holding to that decision.

"Lizzy?" Jane peeked around Elizabeth's bedroom door. "Papa and Mr. Darcy have finished their meeting, and Mr. Bingley has arrived."

Elizabeth took one more look in the glass and

poked a wayward curl into her bonnet. "I am ready."

"All will be well," Jane whispered as she took Elizabeth's arm and they descended the stairs.

"I pray you are right," Elizabeth whispered back.

Jane gave her a sisterly glare. It was the nearly stern expression Jane often used when she was scolding Lizzy about something that was causing Elizabeth unease. "I know it will be well, for we shall make it so."

Elizabeth laughed at the comment. "I still do not know how you intend to do so." Jane had assured her over and over last night that all would be well. Mr. Darcy would love her, and she would love Mr. Darcy. Theirs was to be a marriage that would rival the greatest romance in all history.

Jane pulled Elizabeth to a stop. "How can he not but love you as I do? And if he is Mr. Bingley's dearest friend, how can he be anything less than the best of men?"

She pretended to straighten Elizabeth's collar so that their stopping mid-descent would not appear so strange to those who waited below. Again, it was an action she had done often to purchase a few private moments of conversation with Elizabeth.

"Question everything, Lizzy. I should not have to tell you this as questioning is in your nature, but you have questioned very little, save his honour, since Mr. Darcy arrived." There was a sharp edge to her scolding tone.

Elizabeth felt the warmth of shame creep into her cheeks. It was true. She had not questioned any story that she had heard about Mr. Darcy. She had been willing to believe the worst about the gentleman without giving the information proper consideration.

"There." Jane gave one more small tug at Elizabeth's collar and, then taking her arm, continued down the stairs.

Elizabeth studied Mr. Darcy's expression as closely as she could. Jane had claimed there was a slight smile that softened his features when he looked at her. She did not see it.

"Miss Elizabeth, I trust you are well?" There was that puzzling uncertainty again. The same as what she had heard last night in the library.

She smiled. "I am well. And you?"

The space between Mr. Darcy's brows widened and the corners of his mouth turned up. She blinked. Was this the expression of which Jane spoke?

"I am well." He offered her his arm as they exited the house.

She glanced at him as she thought of Jane's admonition to question everything. There was no better time to begin following Jane's advice than now she supposed.

"You said I could ask questions, did you not?"

Mr. Darcy nodded and slowed his pace a bit to fall further behind Bingley and Jane.

"Just now, when you greeted me, you said you trusted I was well, but the inflection in your voice said you did not trust it to be so. Why?" She studied the ground in front of her. Her nerves were threatening to undo her again. She was certain that such an impertinent question would only increase his disapproval.

They took were three agonizingly silent steps before Mr. Darcy spoke.

"You were rather distraught last night. I worried that you were still distraught today or that your distress would make you unwell. I wanted to trust you were well, but I feared you were not."

That was not at all what she had expected him to

say. It was... well... it was excessively caring. "You were worried about me?"

"It seems I must admit to another fault, Miss Elizabeth."

"Indeed?" She peeked up at him. The smile he wore took her by surprise.

"I have the propensity to torment myself by fretting...." He took a deep breath and although it looked as if it made him exceedingly uncomfortable to do so, he added, "especially about people who are of great importance to me."

She tilted her head as she studied him. Was he saying she was important to him? Surely, that could not be what he meant. They had not known each other long enough for that.

"Such as my sister, my cousin, Bingley, and you," he continued. His neck and then his ears grew red as his shoulders rose and fell pronouncedly as if breathing were difficult while his words settled into Elizabeth's mind.

"Me?" The thought was so startling that she stopped walking. He was including her as a person he though of as important. But why? What reason would he have to care for her? She could not think of anything that would prompt him to feel so.

Unless... Yes, that must be it. She smiled. "Of course, I shall be your wife. It is expected."

It was his turn to cock his head and study her with confusion. But why would that make him confused? Was it not the obvious reason? What could he possibly see to find fault with in what she had said?

"I am sorry, Mr. Darcy. Did I say something amiss?"

He shook his head and gave a small laugh. "No, Miss Elizabeth, but I fear I have."

Darcy regretted his choice of words immediately as he saw the look on her face. Quickly, he attempted to correct her misunderstanding.

"I do not mean I said something amiss just now. I was referring to my comment at the assembly which seems to have left you with the mistaken notion that I could never care for you."

She had dropped his arm and now walked with her hands clasped behind her back. "I do not question your ability to fulfill your duty, Mr. Darcy."

"I am not speaking of fulfilling duty, Miss Elizabeth." He stopped in front of her.

"Then, pray tell, of what are you speaking, Mr. Darcy?"

"I am saying, Miss Elizabeth, that I have been able to think of very little else save you since that confounded assembly." He looked away from her shocked expression. "Your eyes are enchanting, and your wit is enthralling."

"But you claimed I was merely tolerable!"

"I did." He sighed. "I was in a foul mood. I did not wish to encourage my friend in his quest to find me a partner, nor did I wish to give false hope to any lady." He could tell by the lift of her eyebrow that he had said something wrong again. "I am expected to marry well. I thought the people in attendance to be beneath me."

"That was most obvious." Her tone was sharp and firm. "It is a happy thing that you did not find any in attendance to be handsome."

"I never said you were not handsome."

Her eyes were wide with surprise. "You did not?" Her tone dared him to say he had not.

He crossed his arms and glared at her and did exactly as her tone taunted him to do. "No, I did not. I said you were not handsome enough to tempt me to dance."

One eyebrow arched. "You did not say *to dance*."

He closed his eyes and tried to rein in his frustration. "It was implied. As I said, I was in no mood to dance that evening. You could have been Aphrodite herself, and you would not have been handsome enough to tempt me to dance, for I had no intention of dancing."

"I see." She stepped past him and began walking away.

Darcy watched her and silently cursed Bingley's idea to be more open. Explaining himself to Bingley was never this difficult. *This* was like trying to reason with Georgiana.

He hurried after her and had nearly reached her side when she spun toward him again.

"Why? Why did you not wish to dance?"

He flinched at the question. He knew he was going to have to broach this subject at some point, but that did not make it a topic that he welcomed having to discuss.

"Forgive me," she said. "I should not have asked."

"No, no," he hastened to assure her, "I told you that you could ask me questions to learn about my character."

He offered her his arm again and was relieved when she placed her hand on it. They walked along for a few moments in silence as he considered the best way to answer. She was to be his wife and a sister to Georgiana. It would do well for her to know what had happened, but her defense of Wickham during their dance made him uneasy.

"Before I answer your question, I must ask something of you."

When she peeked up at him, her eyes caught his and held them for a heart beat before her lips tipped up in a small, comforting smile and her hand pressed more firmly into his arm. "Of course," she said as if she knew that this topic was one which would cause him pain.

"I do not wish to offend," he began. How did one ask the lady he was promised to marry if she loved a gentleman you despised? Deciding that the answer was directly, he continued. "You spoke so passionately last night about Mr. Wickham. Has he touched your heart?" The words felt bitter. They made his stomach twist, and his heart ache. He was unsure what he would do if her answer were in the positive. Silently, he prayed that it would not be.

"Mr. Wickham?" she asked in surprise.

Darcy nodded.

"I do not understand how that has anything to do with your not wishing to dance."

"I realize it does not seem related, but I assure you it is." He looked at her and smiled softly. "I do not wish to cause you pain, although I fear I will."

She shook her head. "I have enjoyed Mr. Wickham's company, but he has not touched my heart."

Darcy released the breath that he had been holding as he had awaited her reply. "I do not know what stories Wickham has told you, although I am certain they did not paint me in a favourable light."

Elizabeth smiled sheepishly at Mr. Darcy. "They did not." A sinking feeling began to settle in her stomach. She thought of how Jane had cautioned her about believing Wickham's tales.

"He told you that he has a long connection with my family?"

She nodded. "He said his father was your father's steward."

"Indeed, he was my father's steward, as well as a good man. Did Wickham tell you that he was also my father's godson?"

"He did."

"And that my father preferred his company to mine?"

She heard the underlying pain in the question and gave him an apologetic look as she nodded.

"Did he tell you that my father left him an inheritance?"

She looked at the ground. "He said you had refused to give it to him."

She heard him draw in a breath, release it, and then draw in another. Apparently, Mr. Wickham had struck a powerful blow to Mr. Darcy with that bit of information, and Elizabeth felt her shame at having listened to the man grow deeper.

"Even though I did not see him as fit for the church, I refused him nothing at first," Mr. Darcy said calmly, though Elizabeth could feel the anger that seethed beneath "Wickham was careful to conceal his want of principle from my father but not from me. My father, knowing nothing of Wickham's true nature and loving him as if he were a younger son, wished to see him advanced in his career as far as he was able and, to that end, my father made me promise to see his wishes fulfilled. He desired for Wickham to have a valuable family living when it became vacant and a legacy of one thousand pounds."

To Elizabeth that seemed very generous, but

Wickham had neither money nor a living so if Mr. Darcy had not denied him his inheritance, then what had become of it?

"Wickham's father did not long survive my own. Not long after these events, Wickham made me aware that he had decided against taking orders and had some resolve to study the law instead. An agreement was reached wherein he resigned all rights to the living and instead accepted a settlement of three thousand pounds."

Three thousand pounds? "In addition to the one-thousand-pound legacy?"

"Yes."

The amount of money was not insignificant. "And you gave it to him?"

Mr. Darcy nodded. "I did not hear from him again for about three years when he petitioned me for the living that had recently become vacant. The law had not been profitable for him, his inheritance was gone, and he had decided to take orders if I would present him with the living. I refused, and as you can well imagine, he was not pleased."

Gone? Four thousand pounds gone in three years?

Mr. Darcy stopped walking and turned to look

at her. "Did Wickham tell you anything more than this?" There was an urgency in his voice.

She shook her head slowly. There was more? She was beginning to feel quite ill at the realization of how completely she had been duped. "He only told me half of what you have just now related to me."

# Chapter 4

Taking in the paleness of her face and the tears that clung to her eyelashes, Darcy sought a place for her to rest. He continued his story as he led her off the road to a stile in the hedgerows.

"My sister, Georgiana, is much younger than I. When my father died, she was placed in the care of myself and my cousin, Colonel Fitzwilliam. Earlier this year, my cousin and I removed her from school and hired a companion for her. This past summer, Georgie and her companion, Mrs. Younge, travelled to Ramsgate. Wickham followed; I suspect it was by design since we later learned Wickham had a previous connection with the lady."

He brushed whatever dust there may be from the stile before allowing Elizabeth to take a seat.

"Georgiana only remembered the kindness Wickham had shown her as a child. He, knowing she had an affectionate nature, played upon it, and soon, he convinced her that she was in love. His persuasion was such that she consented to an elopement."

Elizabeth gasped, and the tears which had threatened began to slip down her cheeks. Darcy took out his handkerchief and, stooping down, handed it to her.

"I prevented the elopement. Georgiana is well, save for an injured heart."

Elizabeth's hand rested on her heart. A small groan of what Darcy could only describe as pure grief escaped her lips.

"And this is why you did not wish to dance?" she asked.

"It is." Kneeling beside her, he longed to dry her tears for her as he had for Georgiana when she had come to realize that Wickham did not care for her as much as he cared for her money. His heart ached now as it did then.

"I had just travelled a great distance away from where my heart desired to be. My sister's unhappiness at my departure was not far from my mind."

Elizabeth's looked down at her lap where his hand covered hers. There was a comfort in his gentle touch. She shook her head at the enormity of the hurt Mr. Darcy must be carrying in his heart, and she could not fault him any longer for being disagreeable. She knew both what it was to care so for a sister and that she would not be happy to be away from Jane if she were injured.

"Why is your sister not with you?"

"She is with her aunt and taking lessons from the masters. I did not wish to interrupt her education." He smiled slightly, and there was a twinkle in his eye. It seemed out of place considering what he had just shared.

"And..." His lips twitched. "Georgiana did not wish to spend time with Miss Bingley."

Elizabeth's eyes grew wide. "But Miss Bingley led me to believe she and Miss Darcy were close."

"Miss Bingley knows how dear my sister is to me, so I believe she says it so that I will think she would make a good sister for Georgiana and, therefore, a good wife for me." He stood and extended his hand to Elizabeth. "She is mistaken if she thinks I would ever consider her as my wife."

"Because she is from trade?" Elizabeth asked as she placed her hand in his.

Darcy laughed. "No, because she is annoying

and rather dull." He tucked her hand into the crook of his arm and kept it covered with his own. "I have always wished for a companion in a wife. Someone with whom I can have discussions. Someone who has read extensively and has a quick wit. I wish for my sister to have a sister who is compassionate and caring as well as intelligent and strong."

His steps faltered and then stopped.

"I believe..." he paused. "I believe I have been looking for you."

"Me?" The word had leaped from her lips before her mind had fully processed what she had just heard. Darcy stood looking at her with a look of shock on his face that matched her feelings exactly. "Surely, you could not have been looking for me."

He smiled broadly, the light of his happiness shining in his eyes. "Yes, you. I have been looking for you."

She shook her head in disbelief. The world seemed to be spinning oddly today. Indeed, it had begun to spin so last night when he had asked her to dance. Things were not as they should be. He should be pointing out her deficiency, not claiming her to be his choice for a wife. No, the choice had been removed when Aunt Philips had flown loudly down the hall in search of her father. He merely wished to see what he wanted to see.

He was still wearing that same broad smile. "You are perfect," he said softly. "Beautiful, intelligent, compassionate."

Elizabeth was sure her face had never felt so warm. "I am not perfect, nor am I beautiful." She was quite certain that Mr. Darcy was not in his right mind when a laugh bubbled out of the normally dour gentleman.

"For me, to me, you are." He squeezed her hand. "Truly, you are."

Elizabeth blinked at him and shook her head once more. "I do not see it."

"But you will."

She bristled at the sound of such assurance in his voice. She was not wrong. She knew she was not beautiful. Had not her mother said so many times? She also knew she was not perfect. She had just been presented with a glaring example of how she had been willing to believe the worst of Mr. Darcy with no more proof than the words of another agreeing with her feelings of dislike for the man. It was more than she felt she could countenance for one day, and yet the day was not more than half over. She absently rubbed the space between her brows.

"Are you well?" There was the uncertainty in his voice again, but this time she understood it.

"Merely overwhelmed, Mr. Darcy." She gave him a reassuring smile. "There is no need to fret."

They began walking again.

He laughed lightly. "Ah, but I will. I am afraid it is a well-developed fault."

Seeking to change the direction of their conversation, she asked, "Has it been a fault all your life?"

"I am afraid it has. My mother's constitution was not strong. She was often ill, and she never fully recovered from her illness after my sister was born. I believe, I was naturally prone to ponder things more than needed, but when one's mother is ill..." His voice trailed off.

Elizabeth chided herself for bringing up such painful thoughts.

"She was quite wonderful. I believe I got my love of poetry from her. Both my father and mother were avid readers, but my father's tastes tended more to the academic where my mother's were more imaginative."

The look on his face softened, and the corners of his mouth turned up slightly. Elizabeth was so taken with the expression, since it was the same he had given her this morning, that she nearly forgot to listen to what he was saying.

"She would take me up on her lap or, later, next to her in her bed, and read a poem to me and then discuss the images created with the words."

"Oh, how lovely," said Elizabeth. "The scenes that can be painted by the few words of a poet are indeed inspiring."

He smiled down at her. "The economy of words my mother called it. You would have liked her. Everyone did. Mrs. Reynolds still speaks of her with such fondness."

"Mrs. Reynolds?"

"My housekeeper at Pemberley."

A sudden jolt of panic gripped Elizabeth's heart. Her thoughts had been so tangled with her feelings or, more precisely, her lack of feelings for Mr. Darcy that she had forgotten to consider the estate of which she was to be the mistress. She was positive her knowledge of the running of an estate was not equal to the task that lay before her at Pemberley. She wrapped her free arm around her middle in an attempt to keep her insides from fluttering.

"Are you well?" There was a greater note of concern in his voice now than there had been before.

She nodded. "I had not considered Pemberley. It must certainly be very grand."

"It is larger than Netherfield."

"Much larger?" She recalled hearing he owned half of Derbyshire.

"Yes."

Oh, her heart was racing. She both needed to know and wished not to know the full extent of the responsibilities that lay before her. "And town? You came to Hertfordshire from town. I assume you have a home there as well?"

"I do. It has its own staff. Mrs. Vernon is the housekeeper there. Both she and Mrs. Reynolds are exceptional at their jobs."

She nodded. She hoped they would also be understanding and helpful.

"Your father suggested that you and your sister Mary should accompany me to town when I go to get the special license. You could meet Mrs. Vernon then and have a tour of the house. He mentioned that you would be welcomed at your aunt and uncle's house and that your aunt would be best able to assist you in selecting wedding clothes."

She gripped her stomach more firmly. The reality of all the changes about to take place in her life settled in heavily around her.

"This is absurd," she said. "My aunt and uncle live near Cheapside in Gracechurch Street. My uncle is in trade. My aunt is the daughter of a tradesman. My mother is the daughter of a tradesman. While my father is a gentleman, I am tainted by trade. This cannot be acceptable to your family. And my education is lacking. I have not the accomplishments necessary to travel in the circles in which you travel. Perhaps if I just go away quietly. . . if you could help me find a position as a companion, then all would be well for my sisters, and you would be free to find a wife who is more well-suited to the position of Mrs. Darcy." A tear slid down her cheek, carrying with it some of the frustration she felt. The breeze tugged at her bonnet and flipped the ribbons against her neck.

Darcy stopped walking. "You are overwhelmed."

"Yes, and I am unprepared."

"Both are not without remedy." Once again, he squeezed her hand where it lay beneath his on his arm. "We will remain in town for the season. You may begin by learning the running of Darcy House. It is not so grand as Pemberley and has no tenants on whom to call."

"But there will be social calls to make and soirees to attend."

He smiled at her. "You are capable. You merely fear the unknown."

She sighed resignedly. He was obviously determined not to let her escape their arrangement. "When do we leave for my aunt's house?"

"The day after tomorrow. Your father sent an express to inform your relations of your arrival."

She nodded slowly.

"Miss Elizabeth," his voice was soft but serious, "I am not unaware of the challenges before us, but you know we must marry."

Again, she nodded slowly.

"We shall face whatever challenges arise together. I have made a promise to your father that I will care for you. It is not a promise I make lightly. Beyond that, my heart would not allow it. Can you trust me enough to believe that?"

She saw the look of concern in his eyes and heard the uncertainty in his voice. That strange feeling of needing to put him at ease washed over her again. "I shall try," she said, and then noting that his look of concern decreased only slightly, she added, "It is all I can promise right now. I shall try. I really, truly shall try."

"Very well," he said, the crease between his brows nearly disappearing. "You shall try to trust me, and I shall try to be patient."

# Chapter 5

Through the front window of her uncle's house in Gracechurch Street, Elizabeth watched Darcy's coach make its way through the early evening traffic. She pulled in her lip and bit it softly as she considered the man within the coach. As she had promised Jane two days ago, she had questioned everything about him. Yesterday, she had questioned him in regard to his attention to his tenants and his staff. She had asked him about his father and about his steward. She had even dared to ask about his supposed betrothal to his cousin. He had patiently borne all her inquiries.

She was beginning to run out of questions about his character, which left her in an extremely uncomfortable state, for she knew that, now, she must also examine her own character. It would not be a pleasant task since her character seemed to be wanting. How else could she have misjudged Mr. Darcy so badly? A character which had fallen easy prey to the pretty words of a charmer was not one she wished to find within herself, but there it was. She sighed.

Aunt Gardiner placed an arm around Elizabeth's shoulders. "He seems very pleasant."

"A right proper gentleman," agreed her uncle.

"Not at all as you described," added her aunt softly.

Elizabeth's shoulders lifted slightly and then dropped. How she wished she has kept her unfavourable thoughts about Mr. Darcy to herself. Then, it would not be quite so painful to be wrong, for the folly would be one which was only known privately. But that was not the case. She had written to her favourite aunt about Mr. Darcy, and now she must admit her error. "I may have misjudged him."

She turned sad eyes to her aunt. "I do not know who he is. I was so sure I knew, but I do not."

"Ah, my dear. Something tells me you know more than you will allow yourself to admit."

Aunt Gardiner turned Elizabeth away from the

window. "We should get you and Mary installed in your room."

She led Elizabeth from the room and started up the stairs. "You will, of course, have to share the story about how you became betrothed to a man you were so set against. I have had your father's version, but I would like to hear yours."

She turned to the right at the top of the stairs and opened the second door on her left. "Your uncle has brought home some lovely laces and a few pieces of silk that he thought you might like. I have to say; your uncle has an excellent eye for colour. You would look lovely in all of them, so you shall have a dress from each. Mrs. Havelston has lent me her book of fashions. She knows how much you dislike spending hours in her shop choosing fabrics and patterns, and our time is limited."

Elizabeth sat heavily on the bed while Mary opened a trunk and began the task of unpacking. "It is all too much," she said.

"Are you indeed your mother's daughter?" Aunt Gardiner crossed her arms and gave Elizabeth an amused but quizzical look.

A small laugh escaped Mary. "She has been for three days now."

Elizabeth gasped.

"You have been a ball of nerves ever since the ball," Mary explained.

Not without good reason!

"I am being forced to marry a man I barely know because my aunt created a scene," Elizabeth protested. "You would not be a picture of serenity either if it were you."

Mary shrugged. "Perhaps I would be as distraught as you if I were to be forced to marry a wealthy, handsome gentleman who obviously cared for me, but I rather doubt it." Mary hung a gown in the wardrobe. "Mr. Darcy is not so awfully bad. You could have ended up marrying Mr. Collins."

"Mary!" Elizabeth shook her head not knowing what else to say to her sister.

Mary turned toward her sister and placed her hands on her hips. "Do not scold me, Lizzy. Mr. Collins had requested a meeting with Father, and he had been following you around like a lost lamb. It does not take great intelligence to know that he had selected you to be his wife. Surely, you knew."

She gave Elizabeth a pointed look that said she would not believe any protest of ignorance before she returned to the trunk to continue the unpacking.

"I had my suspicions," Elizabeth admitted softly. In fact, she had looked for a means of escape every time she had seen Mr. Collins moving in her direction.

"As I see it," Mary continued, "Mr. Darcy saved you from a dire fate, and you should be grateful." She hung another dress in the wardrobe. "And I heard rumours about Mr. Wickham that would make you blush."

She turned and looked at Elizabeth with another pointed look that dared her to contradict what she had said. "I learn many things listening to conversations while I am being ignored," she added as proof that what she knew was to be believed.

"Ignored?" Shock suffused Elizabeth's face. She had never considered how little attention was paid to Mary.

"Do not mistake me. To be ignored is not a travesty to me. I much prefer to watch and listen." Mary placed a brush on the table near the mirror before joining her aunt and Elizabeth on the bed.

"As I see it, you are fortunate. Mr. Darcy adores you. I know he does, for I have seen it."

"Is this true?" Aunt Gardiner asked.

"Oh, it is!" Mary assured her before Elizabeth could say anything. "Mr. Darcy watches Lizzy's every move, and the look on his face...."

She grabbed Elizabeth's hand and spoke wistfully, "It is like Jane's when she speaks about Mr. Bingley." She bounced a bit on the bed as she tucked her feet under her skirts. "And did you know he thinks you have fine eyes? Millicent heard him say it to Miss Bingley. He loves you, Lizzy. He absolutely loves you."

She turned to her aunt. "Did you not see how attentive he was today? He is that way whenever Lizzy is near."

"He certainly was attentive," Aunt Gardiner agreed.

"But what if I do not love him?" Elizabeth could feel panic at such a thought welling up in her. That was probably the thing that scared her the most about all of this. She knew Mr. Darcy cared for her, though she was not willing to call it love just yet. However, her own feelings and opinions about him were so tangled and indecipherable. What if when she finally untangled them, she discovered she could not love him?

Mary shrugged. "Then, you are a fool."

"Girls," Aunt Gardiner interrupted, "before this discussion becomes unpleasant and feelings are injured, may I suggest we allow Elizabeth to tell me what happened at the Netherfield ball."

Mary looked first at her aunt and then, her sister. "Do you wish me to leave?"

"That is entirely up to your sister."

Elizabeth shook her head. "No, you may stay."

Aunt Gardiner fluffed up the pillows, propped them against the head of the bed, and motioned for her nieces to join her in sitting with their backs resting against them.

Elizabeth smoothed her skirt over her legs. She was not sure where to begin to explain that night. "The ball was lovely, Aunt. The decorations were magnificent and the food delicious. The music was good and, of course, it was well attended. The officers were there, which made my youngest sisters deliriously giddy."

"And our mother," Mary muttered.

"Shush." Aunt Gardiner gave Mary's leg a tap.

"It is true. Mama was a happy to see the officers

as Lydia was," Elizabeth said before continuing. "I danced the first two sets with Mr. Collins, and before my toes had time to recover, I was obliged to dance another with a very agreeable officer before having a moment to find Charlotte. While I was speaking with Charlotte, the strangest thing happened."

Elizabeth paused, remembering the moment Mr. Darcy had approached her. She had been shocked that he had sought her out, but there had also been a most concerning moment of pleasure. She had brushed it away quickly, for she was determined not to like him, even if she did find conversation with him to be satisfying.

"It did?" Aunt Gardiner asked, bringing Elizabeth's focus back to the conversation at hand. "And what was this strange thing?"

"Mr. Darcy asked me to dance, and I accepted."

"And this was a strange thing?" Aunt Gardiner looked at Elizabeth in confusion. "Is it not common practice for a gentleman to ask a lady for a dance at a ball?"

"Not when it is Mr. Darcy," Mary answered.

"Shush." Aunt Gardiner tapped Mary's leg again.

"It is true," said Elizabeth. "Mr. Darcy never danced with anyone outside of his own party at the assembly."

"But he did ask Lizzy to dance at Sir William's party," added Mary.

"So, this was the second time Mr. Darcy had asked our Lizzy to dance," said Aunt Gardiner with no small amount of interest.

"But only the first time she accepted," said Mary.

"I see," said Aunt Gardiner. "Why did you accept him this time and not the last?"

Elizabeth shrugged. "I was surprised by the application, I suppose."

"Does he dance well?" asked her aunt.

"Oh, very well. I have not had a more accomplished partner. However, he is a very quiet partner unless prompted to speak."

Mary covered her mouth, so she would not giggle.

Elizabeth shot her a look of displeasure. "I suppose, it was not prompting so much as provoking." She grimaced slightly at the soft clucking sound her aunt made. "And, I suppose, you could say we argued." She sighed. "I think I injured him with my words at the end."

Even now she felt the sting of his cold reply and the hurt that it had transferred to her. It was not a hurt for herself but for him. It had startled her to feel anything but dislike for the gentleman. It was that moment more than even his asking her to dance that has started her world spinning.

"And then?" her aunt prompted.

"And then I sought a place to think and went to the library." She sighed again. "He was there, reading a book. I should have left and found another place, but I did not."

Her aunt nodded slowly and patted Mary's leg, a signal to remain quiet. "And why did you not leave?"

"I do not know." Elizabeth rested her head against the bed frame.

"You know," her aunt said softly. "You stayed because..."

Elizabeth closed her eyes. "I stayed because he was there," she admitted, "but I do not know why."

"I would venture to guess," her aunt said, "that it was both because your heart cared that you had injured him and because you do not dislike him."

Elizabeth nodded. She could not refute her aunt's words, but it had been more than that. She had felt an unusual peace just sitting there with him. "Then my aunt came to the door just as Mr. Darcy opened it. I was putting on my slippers and smoothing my skirts from having been sitting comfortably."

"And she assumed that more than reading had taken place?"

Elizabeth's cheeks flamed at the implication of Aunt Gardiner's words.

"Yes. Aunt Philips immediately went in search of my father. I would have gone after her, but Mr. Darcy stopped me. He told me the damage to my reputation would be far greater if I were to chase after her. So, I remained in the library until my father came."

"And Mr. Darcy, what did he do?"

"He paced the room and inquired after my health several times. Then, when my father came, he offered to marry me."

"And how has he treated you since that time?"

Elizabeth sighed. "He has been very solicitous. He has allowed me to ask him questions, and he has answered readily."

She smiled slightly as she remembered his look of patient agitation at her copious questioning.

She knew that he had tired of speaking about himself well before she had finished questioning, but he had continued to answer just as he had promised her he would. Today, Mr. Darcy had willingly shared stories of his family while travelling. He had even laughed along with her and Mary when he related how, on the advice of his cousin, Richard, he had come to be standing waist deep in a cold stream making fish noises in an attempt to catch the largest fish. He was not the man she had thought him to be.

"I agree with Mary and your father," Aunt Gardiner said, climbing off the bed. "Mr. Darcy cares for you." She bent and kissed Elizabeth's forehead. "It will be a good match. I believe that confused look on your face and that fluttering of your heart..." She smiled when Elizabeth looked at her in surprise.

"I felt it myself many years ago," she explained. "It is the beginnings of love. Be brave, my dear Lizzy. Do not let those feelings frighten you, for they can lead to an incredibly happy life for you as they have for me."

She stood and straightened her skirts. "I shall bring Mrs. Havelston's book for you to look at while you rest before dinner. We can decide which design will work best with which material after you have chosen the pattern. There are four pieces of cloth, so you must choose four dresses tonight. Then, tomorrow, before we go to tour Darcy House, we can visit Mrs. Havelston so she can begin the work on your clothes." She gave Elizabeth a look that brooked no objections to her plan before she hurried out the door.

# Chapter 6

Darcy placed his hat and gloves on the table near the door before shrugging out of his coat. "I will see both you and Mrs. Vernon in my study in a quarter-hour," he said to his butler. "We will be receiving very particular guests tomorrow. It is of the utmost importance that all is in order to receive them."

Mr. Daniels's brows rose a nearly imperceivable amount, but Darcy noticed it.

"I know it is an unusual request, and I do not doubt your ability to be ready for any and all visitors, but this situation does require explanation."

"Very good, sir."

Darcy turned to go to his study.

"Sir," Daniels said, causing Darcy to stop and turn back. "Colonel Fitzwilliam is in residence, sir."

"Hiding from his father?" Darcy queried with an amused smile. His cousin often took up residence at Darcy House when he and his father were in a dispute.

"It is not for me to say, sir," Daniels replied with a slight nod of his head.

"I am sure he will tell me about it."

"I am sure he shall, sir." A slight smile and a twinkle in the elderly man's eye told Darcy that Richard had already spoken his fill to the butler.

Darcy shook his head. His cousin was not the proper son of an earl. He viewed class lines as a thing of the past and continually spoke of how the aristocracy and landowners would soon be of less significance than a skilled and shrewd tradesman. "Have him join us."

"Very good, sir." Daniels bowed slightly and went to do as requested.

Darcy entered his study and shuffled through the correspondence that lay on his desk. It was business that needed his attention, but it would have to wait. Elizabeth's visit and her acceptance in his family were far more urgent. He placed the letters he held back in the fine wooden box on the corner of his desk and took out supplies to write a note. He was just preparing to write his missive when the door to his office opened.

"Did Bingley tire of your company?" Richard asked as he took a seat in front of his cousin's desk. "Or did you tire of his sister?"

Darcy rolled his eyes at his cousin. "Neither. I have business that needs my attention."

"Does this business require particular visitors?"

"Yes." Darcy dipped his pen in the ink. "Now if you will pardon me for a moment, I have an urgent message to write."

"Urgent?" Richard stood and looked over the desk to where Darcy was writing. "Aunt Sophia?"

Darcy sighed. "I need her to be here tomorrow." He looked up from his writing. "You will understand after I have spoken to you, but this must be written first."

"Very well," said Richard taking a seat. "Particular guests and Aunt Sophia." He drummed his fingers on the arm of the chair.

"I will explain in a moment," Darcy growled, glaring at Richard's fingers, which ceased their tapping.

"It must be excessively distressing business for

you to have lost what little patience you possess," Richard commented.

Darcy signed his name to the note and returned his pen to the holder. "I am getting married."

"Married?" Richard cried.

"Yes, married."

Darcy stood and motioned for his housekeeper and butler to enter and take a chair. "My betrothed is coming for a tour of the house tomorrow. That is why I needed to speak to you."

He folded his note and sealed it. "This must be delivered as soon as can be today." He lay the missive on the desk in front of Mr. Daniels. "I would like for Lady Sophia to be the first of my relatives, other than Richard, whom Miss Elizabeth meets." He glanced at his cousin. "The others can be less welcoming."

Richard laughed lightly. "Meaning she is not someone of whom my traditional father will approve?"

Darcy grimaced. There were few ladies of whom his uncle would approve, for there were few families his uncle thought good enough to be joined to his.

"I fear she is not. Her name is Elizabeth Bennet

and is the daughter of a landed gentleman. However, her father is of little standing, and his wife is the daughter of a tradesman. Elizabeth is currently staying with her relations in Gracechurch Street."

"Near Cheapside?" Richard's eyebrows rose in surprise.

Darcy turned to his servants. "She will be accompanied tomorrow by her aunt, Mrs. Gardiner, and her sister, Miss Mary. They will need to be shown the entire house. Elizabeth is uneasy about the responsibilities she will be taking on as Mrs. Darcy." He could not keep the smile from his face as he said the name. "We will be remaining in town for her to become familiar with the running of Darcy House before we return to Pemberley in the spring."

Mrs. Vernon nodded. "Has she had some training?"

"She has. Her skills are only slightly lacking, but she is quick and intelligent. I am confident she will do well."

"And you say that she is fearful of the position?" Mrs. Vernon asked.

Darcy nodded. "The betrothal has come as a surprise to us both."

Richard leaned forward in his seat. "Were you finally trapped?"

"In a matter of speaking, yes, but she was as trapped as I, and she is not yet completely reconciled to the idea." He sighed as he looked at the puzzled faces before him. This would take some explaining.

"Bingley had a ball. I had escaped to the library, and while I was there, Elizabeth also came in to find quiet. We read for a while, and then I decided to leave. Another aunt, who is as loud and lacking in tact as Lady Catherine, was coming in search of Elizabeth as I was leaving. She happened to see Elizabeth putting on her slippers and straightening her skirts after sitting for an extended period of time."

"So, you were trapped by her relations?" Richard asked. "And she is not pleased to be marrying you?"

"That would appear to be the case."

"She seriously does not wish to be Mrs. Darcy?" Richard could not contain his surprise.

Darcy swallowed. "She does not. In fact, she has suggested other options, none of which are feasible." He returned his attention to his housekeeper and butler. He would explain more to Richard later, but for now, only the basics needed to be shared so that the house and staff could be prepared. "I wished for you to know the complete story in case there is talk."

"She will be our mistress, and we shall treat her as such, Mr. Darcy," Daniels assured him. "And her relations shall also be received with the greatest of respect, no matter their station."

"Thank you. I expected no less, but the circumstances are of a delicate nature."

"Indeed, Mr. Darcy, they are," Mrs. Vernon said. "Is there a particular favourite we could provide in the tea service? It may help your betrothed feel welcomed."

"She has a fondness for almond cakes," Darcy said, "and Mrs. Gerard's cakes are delightful. I am sure they would not disappoint."

"They are excellent." Richard had a fondness for all things sweet.

"Will Miss Elizabeth be making changes to rooms?" Mrs. Vernon asked.

"If she would like. You may make mention of it – most particularly when you come to her suite."

"When do we expect you to take up residence, sir?" Daniels asked.

"The evening of the sixteenth of December," Darcy replied. There was not much time to get everything ready, but he knew his staff was capable.

"I will speak to Mrs. Gerard about a special meal to welcome our new mistress. Perhaps you could find out a few more of her preferences?"

Darcy smiled. "I can."

"Will there be anything else, sir?" Mr. Daniels took the note from the desk.

"No, that will be all."

Richard waited until the door closed behind Mr. Daniels. "It appears *you* are not displeased with this arrangement."

Darcy shook his head in wonder at the fact that he was not. Indeed, the idea of marrying Elizabeth had not given him more than a moment of pause before he had suggested the solution to Mr. Bennet. It was her response which caused his disquiet.

"I wish Elizabeth were more comfortable with the idea, but no, I am not displeased. She is just what I need in a wife and what Georgie needs in a sister. And I need both you and Aunt Sophia to support me in this should your father be difficult."

"Ah, so, that is why you have sent for her."
Richard steepled his fingers in front of him as his
elbows rested on the arms of the chair.

"It is. Aunt Sophia will love her." He knew it to
be true, for he and his aunt rarely disagreed on anything. Therefore, if he loved Elizabeth, and he did,
his aunt would also love her. Darcy could tell by
the broad smile on Richard's face that he was not
unaware of this fact either.

"Wickham has joined the militia. He is in Meryton."

The smile faded from his cousin's face.

"He befriended Miss Elizabeth."

"And you will marry someone who is friends
with Wickham?" A deep scowl had replaced his
former grin.

"She knows about Wickham's treachery. I told
her about it."

"About Georgie?"

"She will be part of our family and sister to
Georgiana; she had to be told. Besides, she had
believed his stories about my ill-treatment of him."
He could see her sitting on that stile, tears staining
her face, and his heart ached to have been the cause
of them – no matter how necessary it had been.

"She was shocked and understandably disturbed by the information."

Richard tipped his head and studied Darcy for a moment before nodding. "If you trust her, then I must too. You do not often err in choosing whom you trust."

"Thank you." Darcy stood and went to the window. "I only hope Elizabeth comes to that same conclusion soon."

"She does not trust you?"

Darcy's shoulders sagged under the truth of that statement. "I did not make the best first impression, but we have had some good discussions. I believe she is changing her opinion of me." He sighed. "I pray she is," he added softly. He had always considered being in a loveless marriage to be the worst fate, but now, he knew that it would not be. A marriage of unequal affections would be far worse.

"You realize my mother and father will insist on meeting her as soon as they know."

Darcy turned and leaned against the frame of the window. "I am aware of that." He groaned. "I forgot to inform Mrs.Vernon that I will be hosting a dinner for your parents and Miss Elizabeth's relations."

He smirked at Richard. "I prefer to be in the position to throw people from my house rather than being removed myself. Now, tell me why you are here."

"My father has been in discussions again with Lord Beacham. I feared a trap, so I am here. And he will still not hear of selling my commission and refuses me entrance to the workshop. Your staff is much more obliging in that regard."

"You still wish to retire and craft furniture?" His cousin had always loved to make things with his hands, but his father would hear of no other occupation save the army. His sons, he said, would serve their king as he had. "How much longer before you have completed the required term?"

"A year."

"Does that mean I can expect you to be hiding out in my workshop for the next year?"

"Quite possibly, unless some miracle of grace occurs, and my father becomes less rigid." Both laughed at the idea. Lord Matlock was known for his firm and unalterable stance. No opponent had ever shifted him from his position.

"You are welcome to stay for as long as you need, of course," said Darcy, moving towards the door. "Now, while I search for Mrs. Vernon to tell her of the dinner party that needs to be planned, you can tell me how Georgie gets on with her new companion."

# Chapter 7

Lady Sophia's toe tapped an impatient rhythm as she waited in the sitting room with Georgiana at Darcy House. She had been shocked to receive the letter she had received yesterday from Darcy. She had hoped that one day, he would finally find a lady to marry. However, she had expected his courtship of said lady to be one which was lengthy and extremely proper. His letter seemed to suggest he was marrying a lady he had only just met, and such a rushed arrangement did not speak of anything proper. To say she was curious was to make a grave understatement. Yet, she was not one to jump to conclusions. Her own son had found himself in a bit of a scandal that was not of his own making, and then, there were her own siblings with their secrets. She shook her head. She knew very well that things were not always what they appeared to be.

She glanced at the clock near the door. "Your brother should expect me to be early. I always am." She straightened her sleeve. "I am anxious to meet the lady who has finally captured your brother."

"*Captured* would be the proper word for it," Richard said as he entered the room. He gave each lady's cheek a kiss. "I did not realize you were coming today, Georgiana."

Georgiana pursed her lips and looked at her aunt. "I was not supposed to come."

Truth be told, it had taken very little persuasion to get Georgiana to accompany her – far less than Lady Sophia had thought she might need to employ. As was natural, Georgiana was just as curious as her aunt to know about the lady her brother was marrying. The girl was just less comfortable with doing something that might cause Fitzwilliam discomfort or displeasure. Lady Sophia had no qualms about either of those things.

"I am sure it was simply an omission made in error on your brother's invitation."

Georgiana looked at her aunt doubtfully. "My

brother does not make errors of omission. He is the most fastidious correspondent."

"Ah, well, that may be in most circumstances. However, your brother does not get married every day."

"That is true." Georgiana's tone was not one of a person who was utterly convinced of the truth of a matter. Her nerves were most certainly on edge.

Lady Sophia gave her niece a soft smile. "He will see his error just as soon as I have explained it to him." She patted Georgiana's hand reassuringly before turning to Richard. "Now, tell me why *captured* is the proper word. Was he trapped?"

"It seems –" Richard began.

"That I am the topic of gossip within my own home," Darcy finished as he entered the room and gave Richard a stern look before turning to his sister.

"Georgiana! It is a surprise to see you." He placed a kiss on his sister's cheek while giving a questioning look to his aunt.

Lady Sophia tilted her cheek upwards for his kiss as she explained. "Georgiana is to have a new sister, and it is far better for her to meet her before my brother and his wife." That was the truth of it.

That had been her entire reason for insisting on Georgiana's attendance at this meeting today.

"But I do not wish to have Miss Elizabeth overwhelmed on her first visit either," Darcy cautioned. His tone was gentle. Lady Sophia knew he was being the excellent brother he had always been and attempting to question his aunt without causing unease for his sister.

"Georgiana is incapable of overwhelming anyone," she stated.

"Yes," said Darcy with a smile, "but I fear just your presence alone will be enough to overwhelm."

Georgiana giggled while Lady Sophia huffed.

"Such insolence," she chided.

It would have seemed rather a stern scolding had it not been for the smile that was broad enough to make her eyes crinkle slightly. Darcy knew that his aunt was not even mildly offended by his comment.

"I am a bit much at times, am I not?" she said. "It is why my brother has never quite known what to do with me, especially now that I have an establishment of my own and the money left to me by my husband. But then, I suppose that is exactly why you wish for me to meet this young lady before your uncle does."

Darcy tipped his head in acknowledgment of that fact.

"My guess is that she is not..." Lady Sophia tapped her lip. "How shall we say it? Am I to assume that your betrothed does not meet with Lord Matlock's exacting standards in some way?"

Again, Darcy inclined his head in acknowledgment.

"However —" she held her finger in the air, "Miss Elizabeth *is* someone of whom *I* will approve, and you wish for me to give her my support."

"Precisely." Darcy took a seat near his aunt. "We must marry. There is no other option, so it is imperative that you give both of us your support."

Lady Sophia's brows rose quite high. "*Must* marry? I admit I suspected that there was a reason for the rapidity of your betrothal, but I had hoped it was due to some innocent reason such as being madly in love, but you say you *must* marry? Why?"

Darcy felt his face warm to what he suspected was a lovely shade of embarrassment. There was no overly gracious way to answer his aunt's question. "We were found in a compromising situation."

Richard laughed. "He makes it sound worse than it is. According to what I have heard, they were reading in the library without the presence of a chaperone, and the young lady had removed her slippers."

"Reading?" Lady Sophia crossed her arms and gave Darcy a skeptical look.

"At a ball," Richard inserted in a loud whisper.

"You were in a library during a ball with a young woman and no chaperone, but you were *reading*?"

Darcy knew that in town, a rendezvous between a lady and gentleman in a library during a soiree was not for the purpose of perusing the contents of the library's shelves. "I found myself in need of a reprieve from the festivities, as did Miss Elizabeth. I assure you, most sincerely, that we were reading just before we were discovered. Unfortunately, I was just leaving, and Miss Elizabeth was putting on her slippers as her aunt entered."

"Indeed?" One finger tapped her arm as she waited for further explanation.

Darcy rubbed the space between his eyes. He had known she might have some difficulty believing such a story, and he had expected a small amount of questioning, but he had not expected to have to defend both his honour and that of Miss Elizabeth with his sister present.

"Would it help you to believe me if I told you that she does not wish to marry me?" He tried not to grimace at the confession but failed. How he wished Elizabeth were as happy to marry him as she was to marry her.

Shock suffused his aunt's face. "You are marrying someone who does not wish to be Mrs. Fitzwilliam Darcy? I had not thought that possible." She collapsed backward in her chair as if overwhelmed by the thought.

"I did not make a good first impression when I arrived in Hertfordshire. I was in a foul mood, and I said something which I should not have said, although it was not meant as it was heard." He cast a sidelong glance at his cousin and hurried on with his explanation before his aunt could ask him about what he had said. "That is not the only reason Miss Elizabeth held for her dislike of me. There were also disparaging stories that she heard from a former acquaintance of mine. Things have been made right as much as I am able, but I cannot force her to like me."

Lady Sophia studied him through slightly narrowed eyes. Her finger tapped softly on the arm of her chair and silence reigned in the room beyond that sound and the ticking of the clock for a moment. Then, she sat forward. "Do you wish for her to like you?"

Darcy attempted to shrug as if the question were unimportant. He did not wish to expose his heart to his aunt or his sister. "We are to marry. It would be best." He knew from the raised eyebrow and the small smirk on his aunt's face that his attempts at hiding his true feelings had been unsuccessful.

"Very well. We will do our best to convince her of your worth, will we not, Georgiana?"

"Of course, Aunt."

Darcy sighed. He had known they would both support him in this. However...

"I appreciate your willingness to take up my cause, but I fear the weight of proving myself must fall squarely on my shoulders. She will trust me less than she does now if she suspects I have given you the task of convincing her of my worth."

His aunt's eyes narrowed slightly again as she held his gaze. "Am I to believe then that this Miss Elizabeth is someone of whom I will not only approve but is also someone whom I will find hard not to love?"

Darcy heard the true question behind her words. "Yes," he said, acknowledging both to his aunt and to himself, once again, that he did indeed love Elizabeth Bennet.

Lady Sophia's eyes and smile softened. "I see," she said, and he knew she did. She had always been excessively perceptive to what he was truly saying. "Then, I am even more eager to meet her and to lend my support to you both, no matter the objections my brother shall raise."

Darcy shifted slightly in his chair. He knew he had to disclose how Miss Elizabeth fell short of his uncle's expectations, but it was not something he wanted to do. Now that he had wrestled those reasons away and had allowed himself to love her, it was unsettling, to say the least, to point out any perceivable flaw. Yet, it had to be done. It was best if his aunt knew exactly what objections Lord Matlock would raise.

"You know how my uncle does not approve of my friendship with Bingley, do you not?"

"Is Miss Elizabeth from trade?" Georgiana asked.

"No. She is not a tradesman's daughter. However, her mother is, and one uncle is in trade, while another is a country solicitor."

Concern etched Georgiana's features. She had heard many of the discussions he had had with Lord Matlock about Bingley not being a proper friend due to his father being a tradesman. It did not matter how wealthy the elder Mr. Bingley had been. A tradesman was a tradesman to his uncle, and tradesmen were a class with whom Lord Matlock did not associate himself unless ordering work to be done.

"Miss Elizabeth's father is a gentleman but of little standing." That was another class of people for whom Lord Matlock had no time. "She brings little by way of wealth or position to the marriage."

Darcy had, by this time, risen and was pacing in front of his aunt and sister. The thought of his uncle's condemnations made him unusually furious. He had endured Lord Matlock's pompous blustering with as much fortitude as he could muster when his uncle disparaged Bingley. But, at the moment, imagining him saying such things about Elizabeth left a twisting, knotting feeling in his stomach and a fire in his veins that spread to his heart.

"A person's worth does not come from social position or wealth, but from character," Georgiana repeated one of the arguments her brother had used on many occasions with her uncle when discussing Bingley. She smiled when Darcy looked at her in surprise. "I would not say so to our uncle, for I am not so brave as you, but I believe it is true."

"As do I," Richard agreed.

"Ah, young, revolutionary ideas," Lady Sophia teased.

"And yet these young, revolutionary ideas are one which, I believe, we learned from you," Richard retorted.

She shrugged and chuckled softly. "Perhaps, but I believe you possessed the intelligence to discover such truths on your own. Therefore, I would rather like to think that I merely assisted you in your discovery."

Darcy could not help but laugh at her reply. She was always twisting things to make her approach to life seem as if it was the most practical way – which, other than being forcefully thrust upon those for whom she cared, was probably quite accurate. To Darcy, her thoughts about how things were and should be were, for the most part, logical.

"Has tea been arranged?" she asked, glancing at the clock.

"It has." Darcy gave a look of caution to his sister. "Almond cakes are one of Miss Elizabeth's favourites."

Georgiana giggled. "I promise not to eat them all."

She held her hand out to him, and he took it.

"I am glad you have found someone to love," she whispered.

"I did not say –" He stopped when she shook her head.

"Yes, Fitzwilliam, you did." She squeezed his hand. "And I am happy for it."

His eyes held hers. Was it so bad to have her aware of his feelings for Elizabeth? Richard and Lady Sophia already knew. His pain would be no greater nor any less if she knew. It was what it was. He nodded his head and whispered a *thank you* before releasing her hand and pacing to the window to watch for his carriage.

# Chapter 8

Elizabeth's eyes grew wide as the carriage Darcy had sent for them drew to a stop in front of a very grand townhouse. "Half of Derbyshire and a good portion of London," she muttered in amazement.

"It is most certainly a fine house," Mrs. Gardiner agreed. "But it is just a house. One with finer furnishings and more staff, to be sure, but a house nonetheless. I imagine it runs quite well now and will continue to do so once you have gotten your feet under you." She placed a hand on Elizabeth's arm. "Your intelligence will aid you in learning the management of this and any other establishment Mr. Darcy owns, but it is your heart that will make it a home."

Elizabeth smiled at her aunt. How many times since last night's discussion had her aunt encouraged her to consider her heart and what it was saying about Mr. Darcy? She had even listened patiently and, if truth be told, with a greater interest than she had ever had before as her sister read to her about love from Paul's first epistle to the Corinthians. She had spent several hours considering what both her aunt and sister had said, and in the late hours of the night, she had come to realize that perhaps the feeling of the tilting and swirling of the earth under her feet was as her aunt had suggested — she did care for Mr. Darcy.

She drew a deep breath and then, covering her aunt's hand with her own, she said, "I believe both my heart and my courage are ready for the challenge."

The door of the carriage opened, and the steps were put in place.

"Though," she whispered as she prepared to descend the steps, "my legs are trembling at the thought."

Mrs. Gardiner followed her nieces out of the carriage and took Elizabeth's arm as they ascended the steps to Darcy House, while Mary walked behind them. Before Elizabeth had time to even pause for a moment in front of the door, it opened, and they were ushered in.

Elizabeth took in the grandeur of the entry.

"It is beautiful," Mary whispered.

Elizabeth could not disagree. The ceilings were high, and the floor shone. The furnishings were elegant but not overly ornate. This lovely, but unfamiliar, house was to be her home. The thought almost overwhelmed her determination to keep her courage high.

She smiled in relief when she saw Mr. Darcy step out of what she assumed was the sitting room to greet them. He was not utterly unfamiliar. In fact, he was a welcome sight. How strange a heart was to so easily flit from thinking of someone as an unwelcome acquaintance to being delighted to see them.

"I hope you do not find it overwhelming, but I asked my aunt, Lady Sophia, to join us today," he said.

His aunt. She could do this. She was good at meeting people.

"Not at all," Elizabeth replied. "I shall have to meet my new relatives eventually, shall I not?"

Darcy chuckled. "Indeed. Lady Sophia insisted upon bringing my sister, and my cousin has taken up residence for a few days." He noted how she pulled her lip between her teeth as she had on their walks whenever something had concerned her.

"You have nothing to fear," he said softly. "I have told them the details surrounding our betrothal, and they are the most agreeable of my relatives. Their support will be invaluable when you meet my less agreeable relations."

She squeezed his arm where her hand lay on it. "I trust you."

Her cheeks coloured slightly at the admission, while his heart leapt at the hope those words gave him.

"Truly?"

She smiled at him impertinently. It was a smile that he had not seen since before the ball at Netherfield.

"Did I not tell you that I would try?" She shrugged slightly. "When I put my mind to a task, Mr. Darcy, I quite often am successful in accomplishing it."

He caught the eye of his butler and tipped his head toward the sitting room. The servant gave him a nod and said to Mrs. Gardiner and Mary, "If you will follow me."

Darcy stopped Elizabeth when she moved to follow her aunt and sister. "You will pardon my surprise, but it was not many days ago when you did not trust me."

She smiled up at him. "I have done a great deal of thinking, and I find no reason not to trust you."

"I am glad of it," Darcy said as he led her into the sitting room.

~*~

After they had eaten almond cakes, drank tea, and had all the usual conversations and inquiries one would have when meeting a new acquaintance, Darcy was pleased to have Elizabeth at his side with her hand on his arm to begin the tour of the house.

"Every room in the house is open to your viewing. Nothing is to be omitted."

She lifted an impertinent brow at him. There was a hint of trepidation in her eyes, but only a hint. She had seemed to take to his aunt and his aunt to her with alacrity. He had suspected they would get on well.

"It is a good thing then," she said, "that I have a fondness for walking, or this could be a very tiring excursion."

He laughed lightly. "I assure you, Miss Elizabeth, it is not that large a house."

She gave him a disbelieving look. "And just when I thought I could trust you," she teased. "I assure you, sir, that this is indeed a large house. Remember to what I have to compare it. Longbourn is modest in size, and my uncle's house in Gracechurch could fit into this one, two, if not three, times over."

"And remember, Miss Elizabeth, to what I have to compare it. I assure you that compared to Pemberley, this house is not large."

"Do you mean to frighten me, sir?"

He smiled at her. How he enjoyed her teasing banter. "I merely wish to prepare you."

Mrs. Vernon shared an amused look with his aunt. It was not the thing to be done, of course, but Mrs. Vernon had over the years developed a sort of friendship with Lady Sophia.

"Shall we begin above or below stairs, sir?"

"Below," Richard replied. "Since I am sure it is the most frightening."

Darcy glared at him. Elizabeth's teasing he relished. Richard's taunts he could do without. "You do not need to accompany us."

"I promise to desert you shortly as I plan to spend some time in the workshop."

"But," Lady Sophia inserted, "you wish a few more treats before you do."

Richard laughed. "You are correct, and for that reason, I suggest we begin with the kitchen so that Darcy can be rid of my presence as quickly as possible."

"Very well," Mrs. Vernon said, "If the lady does not object, we shall begin in the kitchen."

Elizabeth nodded her assent, and the tour began below stairs. Richard, true to his word, left them after pinching a few treats in the kitchen.

"How are you finding things?" Darcy asked as they climbed the stairs to the public rooms of the house. He had been watching her closely for he remembered how worried she had been when they had first spoken about the size of his homes.

"Surprisingly reassuring," she replied with an easy smile that spoke of how at ease she was at present. "The running of the house is on a grander scale than that of Longbourn. The kitchen is larger, and the storerooms and servants are greater in number, but it is as my aunt has said, the operations are remarkably similar. For all that my mother flutters about and chatters, she knows how to manage a household and has passed on much of her knowledge to me."

"I am happy to hear that, and do you like everything you have seen?"

"I do."

He smiled, and it lit his eyes in a way that Elizabeth had noted earlier when she told him she trusted him, and just like then, a small tendril of pleasure wrapped itself around her heart as she once again realized that her good opinion was important to him.

They circulated through the public rooms, followed by the guest rooms, and, finally, the private family living quarters. Elizabeth peeked into each room. They were all tastefully furnished, and the decor was very much to her liking.

As they moved from room to room, ascended stairs, and passed through corridors, she still found the idea of Pemberley to be daunting, but she felt more and more at ease with this part of her duties as Mrs. Darcy. That is, she felt at ease until they began touring the family bed chambers. Then, her courage wanted to hide, and her nerves began to flutter.

"And these are my rooms," Georgiana said,

opening the door to the next room along the hall they were walking down. "This is the sitting room. Over there," she motioned to her right, "is my dressing room and here," she opened a door that led off the sitting room to the left, "this is my bedroom."

"It is beautiful," Elizabeth said. The room was decorated in soft shades of blue with accents of cream and yellow. "It is very like a garden on a spring morning."

Georgiana smiled. "It reminds me of a meadow at Pemberley that is always dotted with white and yellow flowers. It is one of my favourite places."

"You shall have to show it to me. Will the flowers be in bloom when we arrive?" She looked to Darcy.

"They will be," he assured her and offered her his arm again as they proceeded out of Georgiana's room and moved on to the master suite.

"This is Mr. Darcy's room," Mrs. Vernon was saying as she opened the door.

This was the room that caused her nerves to bloom in all their glory for it was such a private, intimate space. "It is very dignified," she said, feeling she must compliment it in some way. It was a very beautiful room. Indeed, it looked a lot like Mr. Darcy. Well-ordered, subdued, and yet, noble.

"Brown is my brother's favourite colour," Georgiana said.

"One of them," Darcy corrected. "There are many colours I favour, but brown is very calming."

"And boring," Georgiana said, earning her a scowl from her brother.

"I think that a colour is only boring if it is not complemented with other shades of that colour or set off by some other colour," Mary said.

"Indeed," Elizabeth agreed, wishing for the conversation surrounding the decor of that particular room to be at an end. "I believe brown is very adaptable as it can complement many other colours. Besides," she said as she moved toward the next door where Mrs. Vernon stood, "both chocolate and gingerbread are brown. I am sure a colour cannot be truly boring if such lovely treats are that colour."

She now stood inside what was being explained to her was a sitting room that was shared by the master and mistress of the house. Knowing that this was to be a room used by both her and Mr.

Darcy did nothing to decrease the feeling of unease in her stomach.

"It is lovely," she said, for it was. She could not fault any of the decor nor the arrangement. If she had been given such a room to decorate, she would have chosen many of the same things. She particularly liked the shelves of books near the fireplace where two comfortable chairs stood.

"You can change whatever you wish," Darcy said. There was that unease again. The unease she had learned about on their first walk after Mr. Bingley's ball. He was worried about her.

She shook her head. "There is nothing I would change," she assured him. "I like it just as it is. In fact, I am sure it cannot be improved upon save for a few fresh flowers in season."

"Through here," Mrs. Vernon said, "is your bedroom and dressing room."

"I had this room redone just a year ago," Darcy said, "but it is yours to do with as you would like."

"You chose these things?" asked Elizabeth in amazement. This room was so different from his bedroom. The furnishings were still elegant, but the design was delicate.

"Lady Sophia helped." There was that hint of nervousness in his voice.

"You have done very well," Mrs. Gardiner said. "Very well, indeed. This is lovely."

Mary ran her hand over the back of a chair which sat near the fire. "Do you not love it, Lizzy? It is as if you had done it yourself."

"It is," Elizabeth agreed. She turned to Georgiana. "Lavender is my favourite colour."

"You like it then?" asked Darcy.

"Yes. Very much."

The smile on her face let him know that she was indeed pleased, and he felt the knot that had been forming in between his shoulders begin to melt. She would be happy here. He was *mostly certain* of it, and at present, he was only allowing himself to focus on the *mostly certain* thoughts. She trusted him. She got on well with both his favourite aunt and sister. And she seemed at ease in his home – their home. Certainly, things between the two of them could grow into a wonderful something, could they not?

"I like her very much," said Lady Sophia, sometime later, just after Elizabeth had left. "You may not have selected her in the traditional way of choosing a bride, Fitzwilliam, but you could not have done better. A gem is what she is."

He watched his carriage moving away from his house. "I believe, Aunt," he said, "that I would have selected her if given time and the opportunity; however, I fear she would not have accepted me." How strange that he should feel so content about being trapped into marriage. "And because of that," he said turning from the window, "I find myself oddly grateful for her aunt's lack of discretion."

# Chapter 9

Two days later, Darcy was in his study working through some matters of business when Richard entered the study with a paper in his hand and a piece of wood under his arm.

Darcy looked up briefly from his papers. "Did you lose your way to the workshop?" he teased.

Richard took a seat in front of Darcy's desk and placed the diagram of a jewelry box on top of the papers Darcy was reviewing. "Will she like it?"

"It is lovely." But then everything his cousin created out of wood was exquisite. Richard truly had a gift for what he did.

"Yes, I know. I try not to design anything hideous," Richard said dryly. "What I need to know is will Miss Elizabeth like it?" He pointed to the design to be carved in the top. "Is this a flower she would appreciate?"

Darcy shrugged. "I cannot be certain, but it does seem to be something she would like. I have never thought to ask her which flowers she prefers."

Richard drummed his fingers on the desktop and hummed as he tipped his head one way and then the other. It was obvious that this gift for Elizabeth was of great importance to his cousin.

"She will like anything you make her."

Richard scowled. Apparently, he did not want her to like just anything he made. He wanted to make something that was liked above everything else.

Suddenly, a thought occurred to Darcy. "When we toured the house, Elizabeth said her room was decorated as if she had done it herself. There are some pieces of yours in there. Remember?"

"Quite right!" Richard stood and snatched the diagram from Darcy. "Do you mind if I borrow one? I can follow the pattern from before but add a few distinguishing features." He was nearly at the door before Darcy could reply that the idea was excellent.

The door opened as Richard reached for the handle.

"Father." Richard nodded to the gentleman who stood behind Mr. Daniels.

Lord Matlock glanced at the wood Richard held under his arm and then, with a raised brow and a pointed look, said, "Colonel."

"For another year, my lord, and not a day longer," Richard said as he pushed past his father.

Peeking quickly at the clock on the mantel, Darcy rose to greet his uncle. He knew that in less than an hour, his aunt, who had insisted on being seen in town with Elizabeth, would be arriving for tea, and Georgiana, Elizabeth, and Mary would be with her. He did not wish for his uncle to still be here when they arrived. However, he doubted that any interview would be short in duration.

"Are you still allowing my son to use your workshop?" Lord Matlock waved the butler away.

No, this was not going to be short or pleasant. "I am."

"I do wish you would not encourage his foolish notions." He waved a hand as if brushing something of insignificance away as he said foolish notions.

Darcy waited for his uncle to be seated before

taking his own. He truly despised how Lord Matlock could belittle his own son as he did.

"Perhaps I encourage it because I do not see it as a foolish notion. Women stitch and net. I do not see why a gentleman cannot carve and join wood."

"It is not done is why. And to compare a man's pursuits to that of a lady?" He shook his head and clucked his tongue as well as any old biddy might. "Preposterous! It is utterly and completely preposterous! But I am not here about that foolishness. I am here about a completely separate but equally concerning piece of news that I have had from my sister, Sophia."

Darcy waited uneasily for him to continue, which Lord Matlock did after taking a moment to straighten his jacket so that all the fastenings were in a perfectly straight row.

"She has informed me that you are to be married, but I cannot believe this to be true since I have not had word from Kent proclaiming the event."

"Lady Sophia is not mistaken. I am to be wed, but as I have said many times, I will not be marrying my cousin Anne."

"But you have a duty –"

"Yes," Darcy interrupted. He was unwilling to

give his uncle the upper hand in this conversation. "I have a duty to see to the proper management of my estate and to see that my sister is well-cared for. These are things which I have not and will not neglect."

Lord Matlock clucked his tongue again and lifted his chin a bit higher, so that he could look down his nose at Darcy. "You forget –"

Darcy did not let him continue. "I forget nothing, my lord. Both Pemberley and my sister shall be well-cared for, and if the good Lord so deigns, I shall have an heir to take my place when I am gone. No duty shall go undone."

Lord Matlock leaned forward and placed both hands on the edge of the desk. "You are forgetting your duty to family position. With your wealth and land holdings, you could have made a very advantageous match."

"I believe I have." Darcy knew, without a shadow of a doubt, that there was far more advantage to having Elizabeth for a wife rather than some lady of the ton — no matter the lady's connections in parliament or the size of her dowry. With Elizabeth as his wife, he would be happy. Georgiana would have a sister of sense, and his estate would flourish with Elizabeth's intelligence and dedication.

Lord Matlock snorted. "Miss Elizabeth Bennet," he said with disdain. "She is nothing. I have inquired about her. Ties to trade. A father of no significance, and extraordinarily little to add to your coffers."

Darcy felt anger welling up and fought to control it. His uncle often brought on this battle to keep his emotions regulated. However, hearing uncle's oft-spouted vitriol directed at Elizabeth made it a much harder battel to win.

"Elizabeth is to be my wife." He knew his tone was harsher than normal by the way his uncle lifted one imperious brow. "I will not discuss your opinion of her," Darcy continued. "If that is what your purpose was in coming here today, I fear you have wasted your time." He stood and moved toward the door.

"I have not finished," Lord Matlock said.

Darcy stopped and folded his arms across his chest. "I believe you have, for I will not listen to any disparagement of Miss Bennet. My promise has been made, and it will not be withdrawn. Elizabeth Bennet *will* be my wife."

Lord Matlock's lips curled up in disgust. "She will not be accepted by..." He paused. "Society," he concluded.

Darcy heard the underlying threat. His uncle was not above spreading rumours if needed to sway the opinion of the *ton* to manipulate someone to support him. The thought that his uncle would purposefully attempt to harm Elizabeth's reputation allowed Darcy's anger to gain the upper hand, and his voice turned hard and menacing.

"A breach, my lord, would be most unadvantageous. Most unadvantageous, indeed. I may not have a seat in the House of Lords, but I will remind you that I am not without influence." He skewered his uncle with a pointed glare. "Do I need to refresh your memory about my father's reaction to your father's attempts to keep him from the woman he loved?"

The momentary look of concern which passed across Lord Matlock's face let Darcy know that his uncle did remember the pressure, both societally and politically, that his father had been able to apply through his sphere of influence. There were people who held strong and long ties to the Darcy family.

Darcy pulled open the study door, indicating that this interview was assuredly at an end.

"Are you saying, then, that you love her?" His uncle stood in front of him, nearly in the doorway but still inside the room.

"Most ardently," Darcy said firmly.

"Love does very little to build an estate, my boy."

"You are mistaken, my lord. My father's estate was strengthened by love — love for his wife, love for his children, and love for his land, as well as love for his servants and his tenants." Darcy shook his head. His uncle's way of thinking was so foolish!

"You have only to compare Pemberley to Matlock to see how love has improved one while the other falters." He saw anger spark in his uncle's eye, but truthfully, he did not care. He knew he was not wrong in this. He had a point to carry and carry it he would.

"How many of your peers have estates teetering on the brink of ruin?" He shook his head again. "Many. Perhaps, if they had married for love instead of position, they would spend more time tending to their estate and less time and money on cards, drinking, and mistresses. It is not love which has destroyed their estates and families but rather a lack of it. Such will not be my lot."

Darcy could tell by the clenching of his uncle's jaw and the narrowing of his eyes that he wished to debate the point. However, Darcy had no interest in arguing the topic further. Some people refused to ever see things logically. Lord Matlock was one of them.

"My invitation for dinner should reach Matlock House later today. I was just approving the menu before you arrived. The dinner is being held in honour of my betrothed. Her relations will attend with her."

He stepped a little closer to his uncle and lowered his voice. "Do not accept the invitation unless you come with a welcome on your lips. I will not abide any disparagement of either Elizabeth or her relations. I am not above having you forcefully, and not quietly, removed from my home if you are anything less than welcoming. Do I make myself clear?"

Lord Matlock's face was a brilliant red, but his voice was cool. He was livid, and that thought caused Darcy's lips to curl upward, ever so slightly, into a faint pleased smile.

"Do not cry to me when you have realized the error of your choice," Lord Matlock said.

"I have no intention of doing so, for *I* have not made an error." Darcy stepped back and bowed slightly. "Good day, Uncle."

Darcy watched his uncle leave. Aside from the anger at his uncle that lingered, that interview had not gone as badly as it could have, and it had been much shorter than Darcy had expected. Hearing a loud "I take no leave of you" and the door to Darcy House closing, Darcy turned back to his study, satisfied that his uncle was gone, and returned to his desk to attempt to finish the work he had started.

# Chapter 10

Elizabeth wandered the room, looking at one sculpture and then another. The detail of each was exquisite. It was as if the men and women had merely turned to stone.

Mary sat with Georgiana on a bench nearby. Both had their sketchbooks in hand and were busy drawing while Elizabeth was happy to just be looking at the exhibits. Drawing was not a talent she possessed, and the act of drawing was more of a frustration for her than it was for Mary, who found pleasure in the exercise.

She smiled. It was a lovely feeling to be affording an opportunity for her sister to experience drawing amongst the Townley collection. It was one of many opportunities she might be allowed to offer her sisters as a result of being Mrs. Darcy. She paused as the name passed through her mind.

Strange how it was starting to sound familiar and not unwelcomed.

"You appear happy," Lady Sophia said.

"I am. I have wanted to visit the museum for a long time, but I have not had the opportunity until now. It is filled with so many wonderful things about which I have only read. It is utterly delightful."

"Are you a lover of learning?" Lady Sophia had already guessed it to be true. In fact, it was why she had suggested the outing to the museum.

The main purpose, of course, had been a public show of support for Elizabeth, but she also wished to find a place where she could begin to form a bond with her. She knew that Elizabeth's acceptance in society and even by Darcy's relations would be difficult. Elizabeth would need someone to help her through such trying times. And as lovely as she thought Mrs. Gardiner was, Lady Sophia knew that Elizabeth's aunt was not as familiar with the ins and outs of the *ton* as she herself was.

Elizabeth gave a little shrug and ducked her head as if embarrassed. "I am, and my mother bemoans the fact on a regular basis. It is not the thing for a lady."

"Oh, I disagree," Lady Sophia said. "But, then again, I disagree with a great many things that are the thing." She linked her arm with Elizabeth's as they walked. "I am a lover of learning, as was my husband. It is a glorious thing when a lady can find a gentleman who not only tolerates but encourages his wife to learn —not just as most ladies do but as a capable, rational human being should."

She paused in front of a statue. "My nephew is such a man. You are a fortunate lady." She pretended to admire the figure for a moment. "I love my nephew as if he were my own son, and I know he will love and protect you with every fiber of his being. It is his way."

She turned to face Elizabeth. "But he is not a lady, and sometimes a lady needs advice from another lady. I am familiar with the ways of the society in which you will be moving, and I would be excessively pleased if I could stand beside you this season as you make your debut."

Elizabeth felt a mixture of apprehension and delight mingle in the depths of her stomach. The thought of being introduced to London society was not something to which she looked forward, but to have Darcy's aunt, the sister of an earl and a countess in her own right, at her side made it seem more manageable. "I would be most grateful for the guidance."

Lady Sophia gave her an approving smile. "I like you, Miss Bennet. And not just because you are to marry my nephew and likely irritate my brother and his wife, but I feel a kinship of spirit."

"But we have only just met," Elizabeth protested.

"One does not always need to know another person for an extended period of time before knowing these things."

They were strolling amongst the sculptures again.

"I would dare say Darcy knew you were perfect for him from the moment you met. He is much like me in that regard."

Elizabeth laughed. "I am not so certain. We spent much time arguing, and his first comments about me were not exactly complimentary."

"My nephew was rude? To a lady?"

"He was not so purposefully. I believe he was distracted by much weightier matters than the suitability of a dancing partner."

"Ah," Lady Sophia said. "I was concerned that the whole nasty business with his sister had addled his brain. It seems my fears were not unfounded."

"I can understand how the concern for a sister could occupy one's mind." Elizabeth felt a strange need to defend him.

Lady Sophia smiled. She had hoped to be able to talk about the events surrounding Darcy and Elizabeth's betrothal. "It is why you agreed to marry him, is it not?"

A bit of colour crept up Elizabeth's neck and onto her cheeks. "It is. I could not bear to be the cause of disappointment for any of my sisters."

"But, you did not like him?" Lady Sophia suspected that such was no longer the case but wished to hear her suspicions confirmed.

Elizabeth's face grew warm. She looked around, but there were few visitors and the ones that were present were a good distance away from them. "I did not know him."

Lady Sophia nodded her understanding. "And now that you are becoming familiar with him, how do you find him?"

"He is most surprising and not at all as I imagined him to be." She covered her mouth with her fingers.

"You have not misspoken, Miss Bennet. He was rude, so you expected a boor. It is only natural."

"Natural or not, it was ungenerous to come to such a conclusion based on one comment."

"Perhaps, but it is still a very natural response to bad behaviour." Lady Sophia leaned a bit closer to Elizabeth's ear and whispered. It was not so much that the information she had to tell Elizabeth needed to be guarded any more than what they had already shared, but she had seen a couple of well-known gossips watching her. It would do well for them to think that she was sharing a great confidence with Elizabeth.

"Fitzwilliam grumbles and snaps when he is distressed. He has all his life. I know he tries not to do so, but his restraint only stretches so far." She saw one of the ladies who had been watching them whisper something to her friend and then both glanced in her direction. "Come. We are expected for tea, and I am always early. If I am not early, he will worry that something has become of me."

Elizabeth laughed, causing the two gossips to

look once again in Lady Sophia's direction. "He does fret excessively, does he not?"

"Indeed, he does." She motioned to Georgiana, who spoke briefly to Mary.

"I believe," she said to Elizabeth, "that you are about to become the talk of the town. Believe only half of what these ladies say. The more dramatic and sensational a piece of news, the better they like it."

"Much like my aunt," Elizabeth said softly.

"And my sister." Lady Sophia winked at Elizabeth before turning to greet the two ladies who were approaching.

"Miss Ivison, Miss Pearce, may I present my soon-to-be niece, Miss Bennet. Miss Bennet, this is Miss Ivison." She motioned to the slightly plump lady who was wearing a deep shade of green and had a rather large feather accenting her bonnet. "And this," she motioned to the shorter of the two ladies who was wearing a lovely shade of blue, "is Miss Pearce."

"It is true then?" Miss Pearce asked. "Mr. Darcy is to marry?"

"He is indeed," said Lady Sophia. "And I, for one, am exceedingly pleased."

Miss Ivison gave Miss Elizabeth an appraising look. "You are from Hertfordshire?" She did not wait for Elizabeth to answer. "Near Netherfield, I understand."

Elizabeth opened her mouth to reply, but Miss Ivison was not planning to let her speak.

"I have had the full story from Miss Bingley. I must say I was surprised that Mr. Darcy would fall for someone of such low standing — not that there is anything wrong with being of a lower station, it is merely the idea of a higher rank and a lower rank being united that is a bit shocking. However, I can see why he would be tempted to leave his realm. You are very pretty, Miss Bennet." She gave Elizabeth another appraising look. "Very pretty," she mumbled.

Elizabeth smiled to hide her displeasure. "I thank you for the compliment," she said. "But I assure you I am not so pretty as my sister Jane. Did Miss Bingley mention her, too? I would be surprised if she did not, for her brother appears to be quite fond of my sister. Which I suppose, if things go well, might result in another lower rank being joined with a higher rank. A fortunate circumstance for Mr. Bingley," she paused, "and his sisters."

Lady Sophia smiled to herself. Standing at Elizabeth's side during the season could be a delightful experience. She had a quick wit and sharp tongue.

"I understand," Miss Ivison said, "that you are fond of libraries."

There was no mistaking the insinuation in her voice. Lady Sophia thought to put an end to Miss Ivison's meddling, but before she could utter a word, Elizabeth had replied.

"I admit I do find a certain enjoyment," she paused again, "in reading." She leaned a bit toward the women and spoke in a hushed voice. "I suppose it really ought not to be done so often as I do it, but books are such great sources of pleasure, are they not?" She did not allow either lady to reply. "I regret that I will be in town for so short a period of time and with all that needs to be done, I am not able to receive callers. However, you must call on me at Darcy House after the new year."

She smiled at Lady Sophia. "You will have to pardon us, but we are late. Mr. Darcy expects us for tea, and I would hate to disappoint him or cause him to worry needlessly by being tardy." She dipped a curtsey. "It has been a pleasure."

"Indeed," Lady Sophia said. It had been a pleasure to watch Elizabeth handle the situation so effectively.

"Well done," she whispered to Elizabeth as they joined Mary and Georgiana.

"Who are your fine feathered friends?" Mary asked Elizabeth.

A small burst of laughter escaped Lady Sophia. "They do rather look like a couple of preening parrots, do they not?" Her eyes twinkled with amusement. "Miss Ivison is in the green, and Miss Pearce is in the blue. They are two of the ton's best gossips."

"And apparently friends of Miss Bingley," said Elizabeth. "They have had news from her."

Mary rolled her eyes.

"You do not like Miss Bingley?" Georgiana asked.

"I do not like her behaviour," Mary said very primly. "She is always trying to elevate herself by lowering others. It is not right."

"No," agreed Lady Sophia, "putting another down to raise yourself up is not right and often ends in embarrassment and disappointment. Unfortunately, it is a common trait within the *ton*, and a disappointed lady with such a fault in character can be very cunning and cruel."

Georgiana smiled at Elizabeth. "I imagine Miss Bingley is very disappointed since she can no longer claim my brother for herself."

"As are Miss Ivison and Miss Pearce," Lady Sophia said. "I fear you will have to face several jealous ladies, my dear."

Elizabeth sighed.

"Do not fear, Miss Bennet. You have already given a strong signal to the *ton* that you are not weak."

Elizabeth's brows pulled together in question.

"You rose to your own defense and that of your intended. News of your defense will circulate. Those two cannot keep a bit of news to themselves even if it does show them in a poor light." She noted the look of shock on Elizabeth's face. "It is a strange world which you have entered."

Elizabeth agreed. She was not unfamiliar with such behaviour. It was, after all, the work of gossip which found her now betrothed to Mr. Darcy. Gossip spread by her aunt, someone who did not consider the effects the gossip might have on her niece.

She shook her head. "I believe it is the nonsensical nature of gossip which continues to surprise me."

"That, my dear, is because you possess what they do not — sense. And," she continued as she climbed into the carriage, "it is why I am so pleased that you are marrying my nephew. He cannot abide the nonsensical and needs a woman of sense which he will now have." She pulled her skirts in to allow Elizabeth to sit next to her. "I am beyond happy to have you as a niece, my dear. Beyond happy."

Elizabeth settled into the seat and attempted to listen to the conversation around her, but her mind kept wandering back to the exchange with Miss Ivison and Miss Pearce. She had felt a need to defend herself, but it was not what truly inspired her to speak as she had. What was it about Mr. Darcy that made her feel a need to see that he was well and that his name was not harmed?

"Oh!" Her hand flew to her mouth and her eyes grew wide as understanding dawned on her.

"Are you well?" Lady Sophia asked.

Elizabeth smiled brightly. "I am well. I was

merely woolgathering." She now saw her dislike for those two women and Miss Bingley for what it was. Mr. Darcy had touched her heart, and she was jealous.

Mary looked at her doubtfully. "Are you sure you are well, Lizzy?"

Elizabeth nodded. "I am well. Very, very well." And, she added to herself, quite possibly in love with the man she was going to marry.

# Chapter 11

Darcy happily settled into a chair near the hearth in the library. The fire snapped and popped sending a spray of sparks floating upward as the flames danced below. Warmth radiated out from the pleasant site and wrapped itself around Darcy. There was such comfort in home and hearth, especially today.

Despite the unpleasant visit with his uncle, the day had been a good one. He had accomplished the work he had set out to do, and he had had a most agreeable visit with Elizabeth. While he was a person given to judging his success by the number of tasks accomplished, he suspected that had his work remained undone, he would have still considered this a good day simply because of Elizabeth's visit.

She had seemed pleased to see him today, and

he dared to hope that it was an indication that her opinion of him was changing. Perhaps, just perhaps, she had come to *like* him. He would not yet venture a thought to consider she could love him. He was not that daring, nor was he about to give up his present contentment just to long for something yet to come. For now, he was satisfied to reflect on her smiles and gentle teasing. He smiled and shook his head at himself. When had he become such a mooncalf?

"You look pleased," Richard, who sat in the chair across from him, said.

"I am." Darcy broke the seal on his letter from Bingley.

"Is there a particular reason?"

Darcy nodded. "Miss Elizabeth seems more accepting of our situation." He unfolded the letter and smoothed the creases. "I do wish Bingley would learn to write more neatly. So many blots."

Richard laughed and opened the book on his lap. "I shall assist you in deciphering if you should require it."

Darcy chuckled and began reading. There was every likelihood that such assistance might be needed. Bingley truly wrote the least tidy letters

Darcy had ever seen, but he also knew that it was because Bingley's thoughts flowed as rapidly as a river rushing to the sea after a season of rain.

*Darcy,*

*You know I am not excessively fond of writing corre-spondence, and since I do not feel the need to impress you with my skills, I shall refrain from discussing the pleas-antries of the weather and how the neighbours get on.*

*I will not, of course, refrain from the pleasantry of mentioning Miss Bennet. She is as lovely as ever, and you were indeed wrong about her, my friend. She likes me well enough to consent to a courtship, a step I thought I should not skip, although those who are considered my betters might deem it unnecessary. I believe I have star-tled my sister with the laughter I could not contain at my jesting.*

Darcy shook his head and chuckled silently. He was certain that Bingley was never going to let him forget that night of the ball at Netherfield, and truthfully, Darcy did not care if he did or not. The results were currently proving to be happy.

*Caroline is still unhappy...*

Of course, she was.

*...and I fear she shall remain so until I can find another of equal or greater standing to take your place.*

*It would be much nicer if she would seek to marry for love instead of advantage, but as you know there is little reasoning with her at times. I shall be glad to pass her care and fickle temperament on to another. Of course, I care for her, and I will always do my duty to her, but I do not always enjoy it.*

Darcy did not envy his friend's position in caring for a sister like Miss Bingley. Caring for Georgiana had brought its share of troubles, and not all of them were small, but she was a delight, especially when he compared her to Caroline.

*Thoughts of my sister bring to mind the purpose for writing — aside from the desire to tell you of my success with Miss Bennet.*

*Caroline has heard some whispers regarding the night of the ball. It seems, from what she has heard — and I only know this from listening to her relate the details to Louisa — she has not spoken to me directly (and I have no intention of asking her about it) — that you and Miss Elizabeth may have indeed been trapped.*

Darcy's left brow arched. He had been trapped?

*The facts which I have been able to catch are that Mrs. Philips was asked to find Miss Elizabeth, and then as Mrs. Philips was looking for her niece, Sir William pointed her in the direction of the library. Afterward,*

*Sir William and Mr. Bennet retired to the card tables but did not play. They merely partook of some punch and conversed until Mrs. Philips came through the rooms searching for them at a very loud volume.*

*I fear, my dear friend, that your compromise was arranged by Mr. Bennet.*

Darcy blinked and read that sentence again. He had been trapped by Mr. Bennet?

*Miss Elizabeth, as far as I can tell and your tale of her distress confirms, had no part in it.*

That, Darcy could believe.

*I have come to enjoy Mr. Bennet's company, and though he may not care for his family as he ought, he does care for his daughters and particularly for both Miss Bennet and Miss Elizabeth. Therefore, I am entirely convinced that he would only do what is right for them, and knowing this, I believe he chose you for Miss Elizabeth because he genuinely believes there could be no better match for her.*

*It is only my trust in your character, which I know would not cause Miss Elizabeth to suffer due to the actions of her father, that allows me to write of these things with any measure of composure. You must know however that I considered carefully whether I should write to you on this or not, for I did not wish to bring you pain or incite your anger. Be that as it may, yesterday, I saw my sisters having a conversation of what appeared to be a profoundly serious nature with Miss Bennet. I fear how they may have presented this information to Miss Bennet and knowing how close Miss Bennet and Miss Elizabeth are, I would expect the information to be carried to Miss Elizabeth with the next post.*

*Do write to let me know how you will proceed. I shall worry about whether my decision to write you was wise or not until I have heard.*

*God bless,*

*CB*

Darcy dropped the letter into his lap, furrowed his brow, picked the letter up, and read it once again. He should be horrified by the news it related to him. His ire should be bubbling at his having been used in such a fashion, and yet, it was not. Strangely, he was filled with gratitude, though he could not quite put his finger on why.

He held the letter out to Richard. "It seems you were right. I was, indeed, trapped."

Richard took the letter from his cousin and made short work of reading it. As he finished his perusal, he looked to Darcy with raised brows. "How *will* you proceed?"

"I will have the license and marriage papers in my possession by the end of the week. We will endure an evening with Lord and Lady Matlock if they choose to accept my invitation. And after that, we shall return to Hertfordshire and be married as planned."

"So, in other words, you will not change your plans."

"Exactly. I see no need to change them." He took his letter back from Richard and folded it before slipping it into his pocket. "I am happy to be marrying Elizabeth."

"But her father duped you."

Darcy shook his head as the reason for his odd feelings after reading the letter took focus. "No, he did not dupe me. He helped me. You must remember that Elizabeth did not wish to marry me while I had begun to suspect that I very much wished to marry her. Her father merely made sure she could not refuse me." His brows furrowed as a rather disturbing thought came to mind.

He blew out a breath. "I suppose she may not be as complacent with the news as I am." He scrubbed his face with his hands.

That thought filled him with apprehension. His

only hope to avoid having to convince Elizabeth that they still must marry was the way she had welcomed him today. Perhaps she liked him enough to follow through with marrying him.

He yawned and stretched as the day caught up with him and the warmth of the fire worked its relaxing magic.

"She may attempt to cry off."

"But you will not allow that, will you?"

Richard's tone seemed to say he knew the answer Darcy would give, and that he would not accept any other. It was one of the things Darcy appreciated the most about his cousin. Richard always sought what was best for those about whom he cared deeply. Darcy was happy to be one of those people.

He shook his head as he rose to retire for the night. "No, I will not allow that. I cannot. Not only because of the situation in which it would place both her and her family but also because my heart would not survive it. I love her, Richard. I do not know how, in such a short acquaintance, I have come to love her as much as I do, but I do love her."

Richard caught him by the arm as he moved past

Richard's chair. "Let me know if I can do anything to assist you. Anything."

"I will." He stood next to Richard for a moment. Then, he placed his hand on Richard's shoulder and said, "Pray that your assistance is not needed," before leaving the library in search of his bed.

# Chapter 12

Elizabeth looked once again at the letter Jane had written. It could not be true. It simply could not be. Her father had arranged the compromise in the library at Netherfield? A tumult of emotions cascaded through her as she read.

...*Miss Bingley assures me she has spoken to no one else on the matter. She has not even spoken to her brother, for she fears he will tell Mr. Darcy, who she claims despises all forms of deception and should he hear of our father's scheming, is likely to demand that you release him from his promise. She said — and I cannot believe I did not laugh as she said it — that she was worried how such an occurrence might harm you.*

*We both know, dear Lizzy, that she has very little care for you — a fact she has made quite evident, since you have been gone, with small disparities here and there. They have all been said, of course, with a feigned air of* concern for you, but she does not fool me. I must warn you. Because of Miss Bingley's comments, Mama has begun to grow concerned that you will not be a credit to Mr. Darcy with your education as it is now and has been petitioning Father for a longer engagement period so that she can instruct you more fully.

Do not fret, my dear sister. Miss Bingley is simply jealous. I would not place any confidence in what she has said. Indeed, I would believe the exact opposite to be true. I would advise you to lay before Mr. Darcy the details of our father's meddling. I believe him to be an honourable man and am fully certain he would do right by you.

If possible, please write to me, for I am anxious to hear how you get on and am not certain I can abide waiting until you return.

Yours, etc.

Jane

Oh, if she had not seen Miss Ivison and Miss Pearce today, she might be able to believe that Miss Bingley had not spoken to anyone on the matter! But she had seen Miss Ivison and Miss Pearce, and they had claimed to have had the whole of the story about her and Mr. Darcy from Miss Bingley. There really was no way for them to know about what had transpired at Netherfield except for Miss Bingley to have shared it. She doubted that such delicious information as her father's involvement in the compromise would be kept a secret and not shared.

Her stomach churned, and her heart raced. She did not know how Mr. Darcy would respond to this information, but she knew that she was angry at her father, as well as Miss Ivison, Miss Pearce, and Miss Bingley.

"How could he?" She tossed the letter on the bed. "Father knew I did not like — nay, despised — Mr. Darcy, and yet he would subject me to marriage to him?"

Mary took up the letter.

"There." Elizabeth pointed to the section containing the news of her father's involvement in the events at the ball. "And this." She pointed to what Jane had said about Miss Bingley.

Mary pulled the letter away and moved out of her reach while she read it. When she had finished, she folded it and placed it on the bed near Elizabeth, but she moved no closer. "You should thank Papa."

Elizabeth gasped. "Thank him? For forcing me to marry a man I do not like?"

"*Did* not like," corrected Mary. "You like him quite well now, do you not?" She did not wait for a response. Instead, she marched across the room, pulled Elizabeth's green muslin from the wardrobe, and tossed it at her. "You have an appointment with Mrs. Havelston."

"For the fitting of a wedding dress which may not be needed," Elizabeth said as she began to lift the dress over her head with Mary's assistance.

"The wedding dress shall be needed."

"But what if Mr. Darcy is angry?" Elizabeth's voice was somewhat muffled by the fabric as it lowered over her face. "How can I marry a man who has been forced to marry me and is angry about it?" It was not possible. She could not do that for it would lead to a most miserable existence.

Mary, who had begun to work on the fastening of Elizabeth's dress, spun her around and place one hand firmly on each of her sister's shoulders.

"Do you care for Mr. Darcy?" she demanded.

Elizabeth, somewhat taken aback by Mary's harsh tone, nodded.

"Do you think he is honourable?"

Elizabeth blinked. "I do."

"Has he not been solicitous of your feelings?"

Elizabeth nodded. How often had she heard the uncertainty in his voice as he worried about her?

"Does he care for you?"

Elizabeth's lip trembled slightly as she nodded once again. She hoped he still did.

Mary softened her tone. "Do you believe him capable of ever treating you ill?"

Elizabeth shook her head. He had not even treated Mr. Wickham ill after the abominable thing he had done. Mr. Darcy was as noble as any man could ever be. But was that not also the problem?

Mary turned her around again and continued working on the fastenings. "Will you be content to part ways with him?"

Elizabeth's heart pinched. The thought of never seeing Mr. Darcy again brought tears to her eyes and her real fear to her lips. "But what if," she said softly as a tear slid down her cheek, "what if, when he learns about Papa's actions, he wishes to part ways with me?" Several more tears joined that first tear in racing down Elizabeth's cheeks. The thought of him sending her away broke her heart in a way it had never been torn before.

Mary wrapped her arms around Elizabeth from behind. "I am not as wise or as serene as Jane, and I have not her experience of years. However, I have spent time learning and have concentrated that learning on books which, I have every confidence, contain truth for living as I ought."

Elizabeth covered Mary's hands where they were clasped on her chest with her own. Once again, she was struck by how often she had given Mary no notice. Mary did not have an older sister or a younger sister to whom she could look for guidance or solace.

"Is that why you chose to read sermons?"

"Sermons and the family Bible," Mary corrected. "I sought truth, and Father did not seem inclined to teach me what I wished to know." She squeezed Elizabeth more tightly. "And I repeated what I had read aloud so that I could retain it more fully."

Elizabeth giggled. "I thought you did that to torture us, especially Kitty and Lydia, by pointing out our errors."

"Well, there is that," Mary said with a laugh as she released Elizabeth from her embrace. "It may not be right of me to say or think. However, as I see things, our younger sisters' behaviour borders on the utterly ridiculous, and it is they – well, Lydia, to be precise – who will be the ruin of us all if her behaviour is left unchecked."

Elizabeth could not disagree with that. Lydia was the most forward and flirtatious of them all. It was not difficult to imagine her making some foolish mistake and plunging herself and her family into ruin. Elizabeth made a few last adjustments to her dress and then, turned to assist her sister.

"What have you learned from all your reading that would apply to my current situation?" she asked.

Mary's brow furrowed. "I would say that it is a child's duty, no matter her age, to honour her parents, but I am not sure that applies when the parent has been deceptive."

Mary looked as if she was seriously contemplating what her response should be, so Elizabeth waited patiently and silently while she finished fastening Mary's dress.

"I suppose," Mary finally said, "that I should remind you to forgive those who have wrongfully used you. Then, I should admonish you to rejoice with those who rejoice — did not Jane share her joy at having accepted a courtship with Mr. Bingley?

And finally, I think I should tell you to consider the story of Joseph. He would not have chosen his lot in life, but God used the nefarious scheming of his brothers to work good for a nation. If the Almighty can do that, can He not also use the scheming of a well-meaning father to bring blessing to you and your family?"

She sat down in front of the mirror as she finished speaking and began working the clasp of her necklace.

Elizabeth's mouth hung agape for a moment. Mary, for all her moralizing and reciting of scripture and sermons, was not so foolish as her father had implied. In fact, she was likely to be the wisest of her sisters. Guilt pricked Elizabeth's conscience. She had neglected Jane's happy news by choosing rather to focus on that which pertained to herself.

Mary turned to look at her. "Do you remember the comments Miss Bingley made days before the ball about longing to return to town?"

"I do." Miss Bingley had mentioned a soon return if her brother could be persuaded to change his plans.

"If Mr. Bingley had left," Mary continued, "would Jane have found such happiness?" She shrugged in reply to her own question before expanding on it further. "If you and Mr. Darcy were not planning to wed, I dare say Miss Bingley would have had her way and her brother would have departed from Netherfield, and our sister's heart would have been injured. As I see it, your situation has already brought blessing to our family, and it shall only continue to do so." She rose and wrapped her shawl around her shoulders, which she drew up and back. "We have an appointment. Are you ready?"

Elizabeth nodded. "I am."

She hoped with all that was in her that the appointment would not be for naught. Her fear must have been etched on her face, for Mary gave her one last quick hug and said, "Mr. Darcy will not wish to part ways with you, Elizabeth. His eyes say he loves you far too much for that."

"Thank you," Elizabeth whispered before following her sister from the room.

# Chapter 13

Darcy watched Elizabeth alight from the carriage. Happiness and dread mingled within him. He would have to talk to her today about what he had learned from Bingley. He had decided, last night as he lay in his bed, that it was best to just deal with the matter directly instead of hiding it and waiting until she discovered it some other way. He was not a supporter of prevarication, especially on things as important as marriage.

"She is here," he announced to his cousin as he tugged at his cravat and straightened his jacket. He had felt unusually fidgety today. Sitting or standing still for any amount of time had been torture.

"And our aunt?" Richard asked and laughed as Darcy returned to the window to see if his aunt had also arrived. "You are not yourself today."

That was true. Darcy felt unlike himself. He

smiled wryly. "If she has had word from her sister..." He did not finish as he heard Daniels opening the door and greeting their guests.

His happy future hung in the balance today. He would do his best to convince Elizabeth not to give him up, but he could not force her to keep her promise to marry him. He blew out a deep breath and sat next to the chair in which Elizabeth had chosen to sit on her first visit to Darcy House, but he had only just gotten seated when he popped back out of his chair to greet the ladies.

Lady Sophia was the first to enter the room. She greeted both Darcy and Richard with a kiss before taking a seat near Richard. "Is he well?" she whispered.

"A bit on edge is all," Richard replied. "He has had some news from Bingley."

Her brows furrowed. That was interesting for that made two individuals in this room who should be resplendent with happiness who were anything but. "Miss Elizabeth worried her handkerchief throughout the entire carriage ride."

Richard grimaced. "Then, I suspect, she has heard the news as well."

"Is this news disastrous?"

"It could be, or it might just be a small bump in the road to their happiness. Only time will tell."

"Does that mean that some scheming to allow them time alone is in order?" she questioned.

Richard nodded. "It would be best."

"Well, then," she said. "It is not very much of a scheme but here goes." She shifted forward in her seat and looked pointedly at Georgiana. "Did you not wish to show Miss Mary your new piece of music? I am certain I heard you say something about it earlier."

"I did," she replied with some excitement. "Could I do that now?"

Lady Sophia smiled. She could always count on Georgiana to be eager to play the piano. "I think it would be wise if you wish to have ample time to practice."

She waited until Mary and Georgiana had left the room, which did not take long since Mary seemed as eager to be gone to the music room as Georgiana. It was a fine friendship that was forming between the two. Mary was quite to Lady Sophia's liking. But her thoughts about Mary and her niece would have to wait. At present, there was another relation and a lovely young woman who needed her attention and direction.

"Now, Darcy," she said with a smile. "I am absolutely positive that Miss Elizabeth would rather take a tour of the library with you than sit here while I knit, and your cousin tells me about his latest creation. I guarantee that it will be rather dull."

Darcy gave her a questioning look.

She shook her head. If only he were as obliging as his sister when it came to taking a suggestion. She would just have to be direct with him.

"You have been fidgeting, and Miss Bennet has nearly destroyed a well-embroidered handkerchief on the way here today. I do not know what it is all about, but if you need to go to the library or some other room in this house to discuss it, then you need to go." She made a sweeping motion toward the door. "However, if you prefer to sit here and have me question you about it, then you may remain, but I do promise to be most infuriatingly curious."

Darcy gave both his aunt and his cousin, who was barely containing his laughter, a look of displeasure before standing and offering his arm to

Elizabeth. He knew full well that as soon as he and Elizabeth left the room, his aunt would have the full story from Richard.

"I do apologize for my aunt's lack of discretion," he said. "However, she is correct in that I would like a few moments of private conversation."

He attempted to smile at Elizabeth reassuringly, but from the way she was biting her lip, he was not sure it was effective. Nevertheless, she rose with what appeared to be alacrity and placed her hand on his arm.

"Could we go, perhaps, to the blue sitting room adjacent to the library?" she asked as they moved toward the door to the drawing room.

He was pleased that she remembered that room. It was one of his favourites for sitting in with Georgiana and Richard.

"We may go to whichever room you please."

"Then, I select the blue sitting room, for it seemed a lovely room for having a conversation."

"I have always found it so," he assured her as they passed down the corridor to the grand staircase. "The last time I saw you, you mentioned that you had an appointment with the modiste. Was it a successful visit?"

"Indeed, it was," Elizabeth replied as they began to ascend the stairs. "I assure you that I possessed no concern that the work would be excellent, for Mrs. Havelston's work always is, but I was somewhat fearful that my order was too large while the time in which she would have to complete it was too small. However, she had all the gowns ready to make final adjustments before adding embellishments. Those which are necessary will be ready before we leave for Hertfordshire, and the others she will have delivered."

"I will make sure Mrs. Vernon and Mr. Daniels know to expect them." He had thought his reply would help put her at ease, but it seemed to do just the opposite. She had once again pulled her lip between her teeth.

"Mr. Darcy," she began as they entered the blue sitting room, and she dropped his arm. "Some information has come to light which may alter your opinion on if we should marry."

"Ah, I take it you have heard from your sister."

She looked at him in astonishment. "I have, but how did you know?"

"Bingley wrote to me. I received his letter just yesterday," he said as he stepped towards her.

"Mr. Bingley?" A deep crease formed between her enchanting eyes. "But Jane said that Miss Bingley had not spoken to him."

"She did not," Darcy said. "Bingley only reported to me what he overheard of his sisters' conversation."

"Oh." Her gaze dropped to the floor.

"My wishes have not changed."

"But my father..." she said, looking up at him.

"Your father is, in my opinion, a tremendously wise man." He led her to the settee near the window which overlooked the street.

"You do not wish for me to call off the wedding because of his scheming?"

He shook his head, but then, seeing her eyes fill with tears, he took her hand as his heart seemed to climb to his throat and yet knock soundly against his ribs at the same time. "I am sorry if you were hoping for another answer."

"You truly do not wish to part ways with me?" A smile lit her face though a tear did escape her eye and slid down her cheek.

"Never," he said softly.

"Oh." She sighed in relief. Her shoulders sank as her posture relaxed. "I was so afraid you would."

Hope poked at him, but he pushed it away. He would rather know the truth than to just hope for what he wished for to be true. He pulled out his handkerchief and blotted the tears which were sliding down her cheeks. "Are you saying you *wish* to marry me?"

She covered his hand with her free one and held it against her cheek where he had been drying her tears. He looked first at her hand holding his and then at her eyes. What he saw there filled his heart with joy even before she spoke.

"I do." She bit her lip and was about to continue speaking when Daniels came to the door.

"Pardon me, sir, but the lady's uncle has come on a matter of great importance."

"My uncle Gardiner?" Elizabeth asked in surprise.

"Yes, ma'am. He is in the drawing room with my lady and the colonel. I have already summoned Miss Mary."

Elizabeth hurried from the room and down the stairs to the drawing room with Darcy following close behind. She stopped at the entry to the room, her hand flew to her heart. In front of them, her uncle was embracing Mary, who was weeping.

Whatever news Mr. Gardiner brought it was not good.

"Uncle?" Elizabeth said as she entered.

He turned tear-filled eyes to her. "You must return to Longbourn as soon as can be. Your father has fallen ill."

"Papa?" The word came out as someone's breath might when an opponent had punched them in the stomach.

"Yes."

"Is... Is he alive?" The question was no more than a whisper.

Darcy saw her sway and, wrapping his arm around her waist, pulled her firmly to his side. He knew all too well how shocking news such as this could be. His heart clenched at the possibility of Elizabeth's losing her father as if her pain were his own.

"I do not know," Mr. Gardiner said. "The message said his condition was grave and all haste must be made. I am sorry."

# Chapter 14

Mary's head rested against Elizabeth's shoulder as Darcy's coach bounced along the road towards Longbourn. Elizabeth looked out the window once again at the darkness of the night. The curtains were not drawn. They were, instead, tied out of the way so that the light of the moon, mingled with the light from the carriage's lamps, could illuminate the interior of the carriage.

Mr. Darcy's coach was bedecked with lanterns enough to make the journey, but Elizabeth was happy to have the extra light of the nearly full moon to make travelling just that much safer and faster. She had not wished to spend even a moment longer than absolutely necessary in London, but she would have been far less calm about the journey if the night had been a moonless one.

She peeked across the coach at Mr. Darcy. His

head rested against the well-cushioned back of the coach and his eyes were closed. However, she doubted he was asleep, for his legs kept moving slightly as if sitting still were a trial.

He had been in constant motion from the moment he had heard about her father. His travelling coach had been ordered. He had seen Elizabeth and Mary back to their uncle's home and inquired after anything that either they or the Gardiners might need to prepare for her and Mary to be made ready to travel. Then, he had departed for Darcy House, only to return in an hour and a half to gather them.

He had to be tired, but she imagined that the circumstances in which she and Mary found themselves were not unfamiliar to him. He had, after all, lost both of his parents. Elizabeth drew in a shaky breath as quietly as she could while dabbing at her eyes. How had he born this sort of pain on his own? She was certain she could not have done it. She was not so strong as some might think. She was courageous, to be sure, but courage only existed in the presence of fear, did it not?

Mary shifted and leaned against the wall of the coach instead of against her sister. Elizabeth watched Mary to see if she was going to stay situated. Satisfied that her sister was indeed going to stay positioned as she was, Elizabeth slipped across the coach to sit on the bench next to Mr. Darcy, whose eyes immediately flew open, letting her know that her assessment of his lack of sleep was indeed accurate.

"Can I sit here for a moment?" she asked.

"You may sit here as long as you wish," he said. There was a hint of grogginess to his voice, assuring her that she had also been correct in guessing that he was tired – likely exhausted.

"I wanted to thank you." Elizabeth placed her hand on top of his. "You knew exactly what needed to be done to have us travelling as soon as possible."

He turned his hand over where it lay under hers and twined his fingers with hers. "I understand the urgency of such a trip as this," he said softly.

She nodded, unable to speak for a moment as tears once again threatened. She tightened her grasp on his hand, finding comfort in his strength. "Thank you," she whispered once again, "for caring for me."

He turned his face toward her. "I will always care for you."

She smiled at him through her tears. "I know, and I will always care for you."

She looked down at where their hands lay joined. "I have been foolish. My father tried to convince me to consider you. He was extremely impressed with your character and told me, more than once, that I was wrong to think of you as anything less than a fine gentleman." She drew a shuddering breath. "I thought I knew better. My foolish, injured pride refused to allow me to see you for who you are."

He reached over and pressed her head lightly against his shoulder. "Shh...rest, my love," he whispered.

She tipped her head to look up at him. "He was right. There is no one who is better suited to me than you."

He stroked her cheek and brushed a thumb over her lips before bending to place a gentle kiss on her forehead. "I love you," he whispered.

She smiled at him again. "And I love you." The admission still made her heart flutter, but not in an uneasy fashion. It was rather a happy sort of fluttering – even now, when things were anything but happy.

His thumb brushed her lips once again. "May I..." He darted a quick look at Mary, who was still sleeping, "May I kiss you?"

He waited only long enough to get a partial nod before bending to place a gentle kiss on her lips. The happy fluttering in Elizabeth's heart increased, and she sighed softly as she leaned into him, pressing her lips more firmly against his while her hand found its way to his cheek and his moved to the back of her head.

Across the carriage, Mary stirred, and Elizabeth jumped, breaking the delicious kiss she had been sharing with Mr. Darcy and began to move to return to her seat. Mr. Darcy, however, seemed unwilling to have her leave his side and refused to let go of her.

"Stay," he said, "for just a while longer."

She wanted to stay right where she was but not just for a little while, forever. She hoped she would have the chance to thank her father for his interference.

Elizabeth glanced at Mary. It would not be the

thing for Mary to find her so cozily arranged with Mr. Darcy.

"Stay," he whispered one more time, and Elizabeth settled back onto the seat and lay her cheek on his shoulder again. The warmth of his person and the fragrance that was him wrapped its comfort around her, stilling her thoughts and calming her heart. She breathed deeply, and he did the same as he squeezed her hand tight.

She awoke sometime later when the coach began to slow as they approached Longbourn. Mary tapped Elizabeth's foot, and with eyebrows raised, gave her a disapproving look before closing her eyes again as Darcy began to stir. Elizabeth gently removed her fingers from his loose grasp and then rising to move, placed a soft kiss on his cheek before taking her seat next to her sister.

Mr. Darcy opened his eyes at the contact of her lips on his cheek and smiled at her. The soft happiness that shone in that smile and his eyes passed from him to her. What lay ahead of her was no doubt going to be challenging, but she knew that she did not have to face it alone. "I love you," she mouthed, causing his smile to grow.

Then, as soon as she was settled back in her

place next to Mary, he stretched, and, when the carriage came to a stop, exited first before handing both Elizabeth and Mary out of the carriage.

The door to Longbourn flew open, and Jane hurried down the steps to greet her sisters. "I am so glad you are both here," she said as she embraced them.

"How is Papa?" asked Elizabeth.

"He has his moments of wakefulness, but he is not strong. We must prepare ourselves, for his heart grows weak." She looked at Mr. Darcy. "He has also been asking for you. I have told him that you would come and to rest while he waited, but he said he cannot rest until he has seen you." She began to move them toward the house. "Do you remember the slight cough he had after he got wet while out shooting just before the Netherfield Ball?"

"I do," Mr. Darcy said.

Elizabeth and her sisters looked at him in surprise.

"Bingley and I were with him on that hunting trip. He was not the only one who got wet."

"Yes, Mr. Bingley mentioned that you and he had also gotten wet," Jane continued. "Two days ago, Papa's cough, which refused to go away, settled into his lungs and was accompanied by a fever. The fever broke this afternoon, just before Mr. Bingley's physician arrived, but it has done its damage."

"But he could recover," Mary said.

"It is unlikely," Jane said.

"But he could," Mary whispered.

Jane placed an arm around her shoulders. "Come, Mary. You shall see him first. Lizzy," she tilted her head toward the sitting room, "Mama."

Elizabeth drew a deep breath and released it as she turned toward the door to the sitting room. "Are you sure you wish to stay, Mr. Darcy? My mother can be trying when she is well, but she can be even more taxing when she is not."

"Your father wishes to see me, and I wish to see him," Darcy said, taking her hand and placing it on his arm. "And I do not wish to leave you to face any of this on your own."

It was just as she had thought. He would stand beside her through whatever came. The fledgling love she felt for him deepened further, causing her to marvel at how quickly one could fall deeply in love once one allowed it to happen. Then, drawing on the strength his presence provided to her, she whispered a thank you to him and allowed him to lead her into the sitting room to sit with her mother and younger sisters.

~*~*~

Half an hour later, Jane returned to tell Elizabeth that their father wished to speak to her and Mr. Darcy. Mary had gone to her room but promised to be down soon to see her mother.

"Is she well?" Elizabeth whispered to Jane.

"She will be," Jane replied. "At least as well as can be expected."

Out of the corner of her eye, Elizabeth saw Mr. Darcy rubbed his temples. Between the late hour and her mother's incessant chatter for the past half hour, his head must be hurting. She offered him her hand and with a small smile, he took it.

"You have done very well," he said when they entered the hallway. "I do not think anyone but I saw your tears."

"You saw my tears?" She had known he was watching her. She had seen him, but she had not thought that he had watched her so closely.

"I did." He wrapped her arm around his and pulled her close to his side as they ascended the stairs. "I dare say you were just what your mother and sisters needed."

The pride in his voice warmed her and made the strain of the last hour and a half feel just a little less heavy. She rested her head on his shoulder as they walked the short distance down the hall to her father's room.

"Shall I wait here?" Mr. Darcy asked when they stood came to her father's door. "Would you like some time with him alone first?"

She shook her head and pushed the door open. She wanted him with her. Always.

# Chapter 15

"Ah, at last, my Lizzy," Mr. Bennet said. He lifted himself up higher on his pillows until a coughing fit gripped him.

Elizabeth removed her hand from Mr. Darcy's arm and hurried to his side. The closeness of the two did what remained of his heart good to see. Hopefully, that closeness would remain after he made his confession.

He reclined comfortably on the pillows Elizabeth had propped behind him. Taking a cup from the nightstand, she held it to his lips when the coughing had subsided. He disliked seeing her as worried as she was, but there was nothing he could do about that, except pray that her worry was for naught.

He took a sip and then wiped his mouth with the back of his hand. "I am so glad to see you. Did you have a successful trip to town? Are all the gowns in the kingdom to be deposited at Mr. Darcy's door?"

She smiled at his teasing. "I have been forced to stand for more fittings than is my preference, but I do believe there are ample gowns left for the other ladies. Uncle Gardiner had selected four fabrics before I arrived, so I shall have four new dresses soon. Would you like for me to describe the lace to you?"

Mr. Bennet raised his hands slightly and coughed twice before replying, "Please do not tell me about lace or bonnets." He smiled and patted her hand. "I know without hearing a word about them that you shall look lovely in each one. Will she not, Mr. Darcy?"

"Of course, sir," Mr. Darcy said. "And I am afraid she will have to endure a few more fittings once my aunt begins her plotting to show her off to one and all in society."

Mr. Bennet chuckled along with Mr. Darcy as Elizabeth groaned. Kitty or Lydia would be delighted to stand for fittings and pick fabrics, lace, and trims, but Elizabeth was more like Mary in not liking to be fussed over. Jane was too pleasant to either like or not like being fussed over. He was happy for her presence these past few days. He knew that her calm demeanor and ability to take charge of a situation had been a godsend to her mother and through her mother to him.

Hopefully, what he was about to say would not need to draw on Jane's fortitude to calm things. She had endured much already.

"Now," Mr. Bennet began, smoothing his blankets and watching his hands do it, "this betrothal..."

"We know, Papa," interrupted Elizabeth.

He lifted his eyes to see Elizabeth's face before darting a look at Darcy. "You know about my part in the arranging of events?"

Elizabeth nodded. "Miss Bingley figured it out and told Jane about it. And Jane, of course, told me."

Miss Bingley? Oh, that was not good. A disappointed lady was rarely a kind lady – especially if she tended to be haughty like Miss Bingley was.

"And you told Mr. Darcy?" He looked between the two faces which bore no sign of displeasure. Could he be so blessed that they were not put out with him?

"No, Bingley told me."

"Well," Mr. Bennet said in surprise, "if so many know, I am surprised my wife has not congratulated me on my scheming."

"I am certain few in Meryton know of the events other than how my aunt has shared them. The number in town who have been informed may be larger," said Elizabeth. "While at the museum with Lady Sophia, who is Mr. Darcy's aunt, I met two of Miss Bingley's friends. They hinted at knowing about how my betrothal came about."

"I am sorry," said Mr. Bennet. He had not considered that his scheming might make her new life more challenging. However, he was not certain if knowing that at the time of setting things into motion would have stopped him. He looked from his daughter to Mr. Darcy and back. "I knew that Mr. Bingley was considering leaving the area," he explained, "and I knew that with him would go not only Jane's chance at happiness but yours as well."

He shook his head and rolled his eyes, for remembering Mr. Collins always made him shake his head and roll his eyes. That man was such a buffoon! "And then, when Collins requested two dances with you and a meeting with me and knowing your mother as I do and having had no success in changing your opinion of Mr. Darcy, I saw no option other than to arrange things as I knew they should go."

"You were right, Papa," said Elizabeth, holding out her hand to Darcy, who took it as he came to stand next to her. "There is no one more well-suited to me than Mr. Darcy, but I was too blinded by my pride to see it."

"Does this mean that you are happy and that I am forgiven?"

"Yes, I am very happy." Elizabeth looked up at Darcy with a smile that spoke of the truth of her words and eased Mr. Bennet's mind. The way the gentleman replied to Elizabeth with a smile of his own, eased Mr. Bennet's mind further.

He rubbed his chest and attempted to hide a grimace. "Then, I shall rest more easily." He leaned back more fully into his pillows. "I assume by your presence at my side that they have told you my condition is not good?"

Elizabeth's free hand covered her father's. "They have."

"They may be right, or they may be wrong. No one, not even Bingley's doctor, is all-knowing." He coughed as he attempted to take a less shallow breath. "However, in the event that I fail in proving the doctor wrong, there are some things which I must ask of you." He looked at Darcy. "Bring a chair. No need to stand for the full interview, my boy. Bring it over next to Lizzy, so you may continue to hold her hand."

Elizabeth clung to Darcy's hand for a moment as he began to move to do as instructed before their fingers parted. Ah, the felicity between the two delighted Mr. Bennet. He would be glad to tell Sir William that he had been correct in predicting his daughter's happiness.

"Now," he said as Darcy took his seat, "about your sisters, Lizzy. Your mother will not be penniless, but her funds will be diminished after Collins receives his inheritance. Do not allow her to force any of my daughters to marry that man. He is utterly without sense as his father was, and I would prefer the entail to die with him. But even a man without sense appears a good option to many ladies when he has an estate."

A bout of coughing followed his firm statements, and Elizabeth once again offered him a drink, which he readily accepted. "I have told Mary already that I forbid her to marry that man. I have told your mother of my wishes as well, but when she is in a fit of nerves, she remembers very little and can only look for an escape."

He tightened his grip on Elizabeth's hand and looked at Darcy. "Mr. Bingley has declared his intention to eventually marry Jane. Do not let Collins attempt to dissuade him or deny him. Do not let Collins have any say over my daughters' futures. He may inherit my estate — what is it but stuff and money — but I shall not hand over to him those things which are of highest importance. Do I ask too much of you and Mr. Bingley to see to their care and futures?"

Mr. Darcy's expression was serious, but his eyes were kind. He was just as fine a gentleman as Mr. Bennet had thought him to be. He proved it further when he replied.

"I cannot speak for Mr. Bingley, though I suspect he will be in agreement with me in saying that it would be an honour to serve you in this way."

Mr. Bennet sighed for a heavy weight had been lifted from him. "I shall have Mr. Philips show you the papers tomorrow, and you will see that with proper management there are ample funds to maintain a modest establishment for my wife whether here near her sister or in town near her brother. She does not have to intrude upon your homes, though she might insist it is absolutely necessary." He chuckled and then coughed.

"You should rest, Papa," Elizabeth said as she returned the cup to the nightstand after she had seen him take another sip from it. "Mr. Darcy and I shall see to the care of my sisters and my mother. Jane shall be happy with Mr. Bingley, and I shall be happy with Mr. Darcy. And you shall grow strong and disappoint Mr. Collins with your obstinate refusal to allow him his inheritance." She leaned forward and kissed him on the forehead. "I love you."

"And I, you, Lizzy." Tears gathered as he wrapped her in his embrace for a moment before kissing her cheek and letting her rise to leave. He caught her hand before she could escape. "Tell your sisters of my love for them and my pride in having been their father. Tell them often, for I have not told them enough." He dropped her hand and settled down into his pillows.

"Until the morning," she said, giving him one more kiss.

~*~*~

Elizabeth wrapped her robe tightly around herself and took the candle from the stand next to her bed. She had tried to sleep, but she had not succeeded. The sound of coughing that she heard as she slipped into the hallway reassured her that her father was still alive, but it also meant he was not sleeping – at least, not as he should.

She crept down the stairs as quietly as she could, taking care to avoid the squeaky seventh step but forgetting that the third one creaked slightly as well. She stood still and listened to see if she had caused anyone to rise to investigate the sound. Satisfied that she had not disturbed anyone, she continued on her way to her father's study.

She paused as she noticed a faint glow of light under the door. She pushed the door open. Mary sat in her father's chair, wrapping a wisp of hair around her finger, and studying the books and curiosities that lined the shelves.

"I wanted to sit with him, but I dared not disturb him if he was asleep," she explained as Elizabeth drew near. "I cannot sleep knowing..."

"Neither could I." Elizabeth placed her candle on the desk and motioned for Mary to slide over so that they could both sit in the large chair. She wrapped an arm around her sister as she snuggled in next to her. "He is coughing, which I will take as a good sign."

"Do you remember when he planted that ivy and placed it up on the very top shelf?" asked Mary.

"I do," said Elizabeth. "Mama was not pleased to have it there. She claimed it would not survive, and then she complained loudly that it was too high to be properly tended, which is why there is now a ladder in here."

"This room is so filled with memories," Mary whispered. "I have always loved this room; though, I never spent as much time in here as you did."

Elizabeth squeezed her tight. "He would have allowed you to spend time in here, too, if you had asked."

"I know," said Mary. "I wish I had."

They sat for a moment, each lost in her own thoughts.

"What do you suppose will become of all these memories when Mr. Collins takes possession?" Mary asked.

Elizabeth sighed. "If we are fortunate, they will be boxed up and given to us, but if we are not fortunate, well, I do not like to think of that." She stroked Mary's hair. "I will ask Mr. Darcy to speak to Mr. Collins. I think our cousin will listen to Lady Catherine's nephew."

Mary giggled softly. "He is overly fond of his patroness, is he not?"

"Mmm hmm," Elizabeth agreed. "Some people are enamoured by wealth and position."

"What will become of us?" The question was barely a whisper.

"I will marry Mr. Darcy, and Jane will marry Mr. Bingley. And you will come to stay with me, and I will put you in the way of many fine gentlemen, and you will find your own happiness."

"And what of Mama and Kitty and Lydia?"

"Oh, we shall find them a small house with servants enough to tend them, and then once you are settled, we shall both assist Kitty, but Lydia may need to rely on Mr. Bingley, for I believe he has a greater tolerance for loud and demanding sisters than Mr. Darcy does."

Mary giggled again. "How is it, Lizzy, that you can find laughter at a time such as this? I can find only gloom, but you, you bring brightness."

Elizabeth rested her chin on top of Mary's hair. "If I did not seek laughter, I would be consumed by the gloom. It is not that I do not feel it. I just am not strong enough to endure it, so I push it away with a laugh when it becomes too enveloping."

Some while later, Elizabeth stirred when she felt a kiss on her cheek.

"Sleep," Mr. Darcy whispered. "Your father is resting well, and it will soon be morning when you may take my place at his side."

"You have been sitting with him?" she asked drowsily, her eyes refusing to stay open.

"I have, except for when I heard a creak on the stairs and saw you were here," he said as he tucked a blanket, which he must have brought with him, around her. "Rest, my love." He kissed her cheek once more and then lit a low flame in a lamp before snuffing out her candle and leaving the room.

# Chapter 16

Five days later, Elizabeth leaned her head back against the wing of the chair next to her father's bed and closed her eyes. The book she had been attempting to read lay discarded on her lap. Her father was breathing evenly, if still shallowly. His colour was beginning to return even if he could not move very much or draw a full breath without coughing. Still, his small improvements were enough for her to allow her heart to hope that he would recover, contrary to what the doctor said.

Behind her, the door nicked open and stocking-clad feet padded softly across the room. She smiled for she knew who it was without looking. Mr. Darcy had insisted on removing his boots and wearing slippers around Longbourn when he called so that he could easily slip out of them when he entered Mr. Bennet's room. His ways of helping to care for her father were so gentle and considerate. He had made certain that Mr. Bennet had everything he might need for his comfort and treatment, and if there had remained any part of Elizabeth's heart that had not already been his, Mr. Darcy's care for her father had claimed it. She knew without a flicker of a doubt that her heart was now, and would always remain, completely his. He was, as Jane had proclaimed him nearly three weeks ago, the best of men.

Darcy took the book from her lap and placed her ribbon between the pages before closing it and laying it softly on the nightstand. Then, taking her hand and after placing a kiss on it, he drew her to her feet. "Come, my love," he whispered. "Let your father sleep. Sally will call us if we are needed."

It was then that Elizabeth noticed the maid, whom he had sent for from London, taking up a place near the window where she would best be able to see the stitching she was doing.

Elizabeth turned her attention back to her father and saw his eyes snap shut. It was not the first time that she had caught him peeking at her and Mr. Darcy when she thought he was sleeping. His expression now – the small smile on his lips and the absence of any worried lines – was one of peaceful happiness just as it had been on each other occasion.

She placed her hand on his, gave it a little squeeze, and whispered, "Rest. All will be well," before leaving the room with Mr. Darcy.

Upon reaching the hallway, Mr. Darcy slid his feet into his slippers and then, with a look up and down the hallway, drew Elizabeth to him, wrapping her in his arms tightly and kissing her.

"Your father seems to improve daily," he said as he released her. "He may indeed prove the doctor wrong."

"But there is no guarantee until the cough leaves, and he is able to get out of bed," she said as they began to descend the stairs.

"There is no guarantee even then," he cautioned.

Hearing that uncertain tone in his voice which meant he was fretting about her, she said, "Do not worry. I am fully aware that my father may leave us at any time. I just prefer to look for the glimmer of hope because, without it, the gloom of melancholy is too easily all-consuming."

"Indeed, it is," he agreed, and then, drew her to a

stop as a loud and unfriendly voice reached them. "My dear, do you remember that I said I have relatives who will be less welcoming and how I wished to be married by special license because of my aunt Lady Catherine?"

Elizabeth nodded.

"I believe I hear my aunt in the sitting room."

"I said I must see my nephew," the voice of Lady Catherine carried to the hallway.

He grimaced. "I am sorry. It will be unpleasant."

Despite how her heart was beating wildly, Elizabeth gave him a small smile that she hoped was reassuring. There was no need to cause him further distress by allowing her nerves to be put on display. He looked concerned enough without adding her anxiety to his.

Gathering her courage on behalf of both herself and him, she said softly, "I will still love you."

He smiled at that, and the furrow between his eyes disappeared.

"You are no more in control of what your relations do or say than I am of mine. Come," she tugged on his arm, "we shall face this together."

"This is a very small room," Lady Catherine was saying as they entered the sitting room.

"Aunt Catherine," Darcy greeted with a small bow. "This is an unexpected and poorly timed surprise." He led Elizabeth to a settee and took a seat next to her. "Forgive me if I repeat something you have already been told, but, the gentleman of the house, Mr. Bennet is ill, and visitors are being limited." His tone was as cool as a frosty autumn morning.

Lady Catherine huffed, and Elizabeth wondered at the near incivility that Darcy showed her.

"I have no intention of staying for long," she replied in a tone that was even colder than the one Darcy had used, "but I must speak with you."

"If that is the case, allow me to tell you what you wish to know so that you can be on your way without delay. I am getting married, but it is not to Anne."

"It is true?" She looked down her nose at Elizabeth, assessing and appraising her with a sweep of her eyes, before returning her haughty glare back to Mr. Darcy. "My brother told me you would not do your duty to your family. Of course, I did not believe him, but now that I see you with my own eyes, I can say I am as shocked and disappointed as he."

His aunt was as Mr. Darcy had said – unpleasant. Next to her, Mr. Darcy sighed as if utterly exasperated, and likely he was if this was how his aunt always behaved.

"I will tell you what I told him. I am not forgetting my duty. My estate is not forgotten, my sister is well-cared for, and my family name is respected within society and will remain so."

Lady Catherine drew herself up a bit straighter in her chair. "Am I to understand then that you insist on marrying beneath you?"

Darcy took Elizabeth's hand, and she gave it a supportive squeeze. While she did not relish being thought of as beneath anyone, she knew that there were those who would consider he as such. Were not Miss Bingley and her friends proof of that?

"I do not marry beneath me. Miss Elizabeth is a gentleman's daughter, and I am a gentleman's son. In this, we are equal."

Indignation at being contradicted seemed to radiate from Lady Catherine. "But what of her mother?" she scoffed.

Mrs. Bennet gave a small gasp. Elizabeth glanced in her direction. Anger flickered in her mother's eyes.

"Do not think me ignorant of who her mother's father is," Lady Catherine continued in the same ridiculing tone.

"And do not think me ignorant of who your true father is," Mrs. Bennet snapped.

All eyes turned toward her.

"I have heard the stories," she explained. "There is some question regarding the legitimacy of the previous Lord Matlock's children. A tradesman for a father is far superior to a groomsman, is it not?"

Darcy blinked, and his mouth hung open. He had not heard the story of those rumours for years and had thought them forgotten.

Mrs. Bennet shrugged and smiled cunningly, causing Darcy to re-evaluate his first impressions of her. Apparently, the matron of the Bennet family was more than just flighty thoughts about parties and seeing her daughters married well. At present, her expression reminded him of Miss Bingley when she was about to be catty towards some unsuspecting lady.

"A certain groomsman came to work for my father after he was dismissed from his position at Matlock," she said with a frigid sort of calm that was somewhat frightening to a fellow like Darcy who had not thought her capable of such.

"Until today," she continued, "I had thought the stories I heard about why he was dismissed to be fanciful tales. However..."

Her smile turned from cunning to something more cutting. It was the sort of smile that hid social death behind a veneer of friendliness. Darcy was certain he had not seen any lady of the *ton* wear that expression better than his future mother-in-law.

"I must say that your colouring is much more like his than it is like the previous Lord Matlock's." She rose from her seat, standing about two inches taller than Darcy had seen her stand before, and called for tea. "It seems, my lady, that we have both risen above where we started our lives."

This was followed by a flutter of lashes and a sympathetic look for Lady Catherine.

"You would do better to find the son of a peer or even the second son of a peer to marry your daughter. Oh, Mr. Darcy is rich enough to be sure, and I do not doubt he has well-respected connections. However, as any good mother knows, if you truly wish to purge the taint of lineage from your family and your daughter, there is no better way to do it than to mix her blood with the blood of a peer." Having rung the bell for tea, she had returned to her seat.

Lady Catherine sputtered. "There is no truth to the rumours. My father was Lord Matlock."

"Oh, my lady," Mrs. Bennet cajoled, "there is truth to the story. Do you remember from the stories that were passed around that there was a particular object which was given to the young groomsman by your mother? I know that detail was not reported in any papers, but that does not mean I have not seen this object or heard the story behind it from the man himself. I have even seen the accompanying note, written in your mother's hand. So, unless you wish to have this particular part of the story circulated once again and with such evidence as I know there is to support it, I suggest you rethink your objection to my daughter marrying your nephew."

Neither Darcy nor Elizabeth nor any other occupant of the room said a word. The composed and calculating woman who stood and began to pour tea was not the woman any of them had come to know as Mrs. Bennet. And it seemed she was not yet done defending her daughter, for she looked at Lady Catherine and asked, "Do you prefer your tea with one sugar and no milk as your mother did or with milk and no sugar as your true father did?"

Lady Catherine's eyes grew wide and her face blanched. "I do not have time for tea. I must continue on to London before the day is too far gone." She rose with more haste than was her usual habit and began to make her way to the door.

"Allow me to see you out," Darcy offered.

She waved him away. "I am capable of seeing myself to my coach. You stay and take tea with your new family. I shall expect to see you in the spring as always, and you may bring your wife." And with a small nod of her head to Elizabeth and to Mrs. Bennet, she was gone.

Mrs. Bennet stared at the door for some time after it closed; then, turning to the still silent room, she said excitedly, "Oh, my, a real lady and in my sitting room. I never thought I would see the day that that would happen."

She continued to pour tea. "Of course, the meeting did not go as I would have thought it should, but a lady can only abide so much disparagement of her home and family before she rises to their defense."

She handed a cup of tea to Elizabeth.

"I do hope you will forgive me for speaking to your aunt so," she said to Darcy before taking her seat, "but it really was outside of enough."

"It really was," Darcy agreed, lifting his cup in salute to her, which made her titter.

Silently, Mrs. Bennet sipped her tea and then studied her cup for a few moments before rising to quit the room. "I shall check on your father," she said as she placed her cup on the tea tray.

"He is probably sleeping, Mama," Elizabeth said.

"Then, I shall watch him sleep," she said, pulling the door closed behind her.

# Chapter 17

"Shall the rest of us take a walk?" Darcy asked when he had finished his tea.

"Oh, yes," Lydia said. "I have had enough of sitting and watching and waiting for horrible news. A walk would be most welcome, would it not, Kitty?"

"We mustn't go far," Kitty replied quietly.

She appeared to be the more sensitive of the two youngest Bennets. Or, perhaps, Darcy amended, she just showed it in a softer fashion than Miss Lydia. Either way, he knew that a change of scenery was just what was needed. As Miss Lydia had said, just sitting and waiting for horrible news was dreadful.

"We will stay close to the house," Darcy assured her. "A short stroll down the lane or a meander through the garden should satisfy, but the fresh air will be beneficial."

Miss Bennet readily agreed and instructed her sisters to get their things. "I will bring your pelisse, Lizzy. I would not wish for you to abandon Mr. Darcy altogether." She was just about to leave the room when something caught her eye through the window. "I shall be but a moment," she said as she darted out of the door.

Darcy chuckled as he saw Bingley riding up the lane. "Do you know that at one time I thought your sister did not care for him?"

Elizabeth looked surprised at the confession. "Did you indeed? I had thought it obvious from their first meeting that she adored him."

Darcy shrugged. "I also thought you liked me well before you did. Therefore, it seems when it comes to Bennet ladies, my skills of observation are of little use." He stood and offered her a hand to assist her from her seat.

"It would appear that way, sir, but I do hope your skills improve upon acquaintance with us."

"I believe they have." They walked to the hall to await Jane, but she was already hurrying down the stairs, calling over her shoulder to the others to be quick.

"Papa will no longer be sleeping with noise such

as that," Elizabeth scolded as she took her pelisse from Jane.

"I was not so very loud," Jane protested. "And the house will be as still as a church on a Monday just as soon as we are out of doors." She stood at the bottom of the stairs, tapping her toe impatiently.

"I am afraid you have discovered our family's most guarded secret. Jane is not always the picture of serenity," Elizabeth whispered to Darcy, who had been watching the proceeding with amusement while he put on his boots.

Miss Bennet gave a small huff and glared at Elizabeth. "If Mr. Darcy were not here, you would be as impatient as I am." She smiled and surprised Darcy with an impertinent look. "At least, now that she likes you that is."

Darcy laughed softly. "I imagine Miss Elizabeth used to be just as impatient as you are now while she waited for me to leave. However did you abide those days at Netherfield, my dear?"

"It was not easy," Elizabeth said with a laugh.

"Ah," Darcy said. "That is why you were so often in the library. You were seeking solace." He noted how she bit her lip as she agreed. "Forgive me for mentioning that particular room," he whispered.

"It is not that," she whispered in reply. Then, she took his arm and moved toward the door. "We shall wait for you outside, Jane," she said as she opened the door. "Mr. Bingley, it is good to see you."

She pulled Darcy out the door and away from the house, and though he was confused and curious, he willingly followed.

"I have come to realize something," she said when she finally stopped and turned toward him. "My father may say many nonsensical things because they are fun to say, but he also says some things which are very wise."

"Such as?" Darcy was unsure of where this conversation was leading, but his curiosity was most certainly aroused more now than it had been when she pulled him from the house.

"He has often told me 'Your feet will take you where your heart leads even if your head does not know it.'"

Darcy's brow furrowed in confusion which caused her smile to broaden.

"For instance," she continued, "if I am upset and

begin wandering while thinking, my feet will inevitably take me to a favourite vista or a place where I can find what my heart needs to make sense of whatever it is which is troubling it."

While one of Darcy's eyebrows arched of its own accord as the meaning of her father's saying started to become clear, a faint blush crept onto her cheeks.

"My heart was leading me to the library because that is where it would find you. It is as you said on our first walk. I was searching for you."

She took his arm and began walking as her sisters and Mr. Bingley exited the house. "I thought it a strange thing for you to have said at the time. How could someone look for someone whom they did not know existed? But then, I was reminded of what my father said, and it began to make sense."

He glanced over his shoulder to where the others walked. "And where do your feet and heart desire to take you today?"

"Here. Right here with you, and in a week's time they will happily go with you to London. They shall endure the balls and soirees, as well as the disapproving relations. My heart shall be happy as long as it is with you." She smiled up at him impertinently. "Although, it may occasionally require a respite in a quiet library."

"It is then an incredibly happy fact that I have two such libraries." He lifted her hand and kissed it.

At that moment, as they rounded a bend in the lane, a gentleman on horseback called out to Darcy, causing him to sigh.

"It seems that today is the day for unexpected visits from my family." He nodded in the direction of the horse and rider who approached. "My cousin, the Earl Rycroft."

"Is he friendly?" Elizabeth asked.

Darcy chuckled. Rycroft would be shocked to be thought of as anything but amiable.

"Rycroft is nothing like Lady Catherine or Lord Matlock. He is Lady Sophia's son, and yes, he is very friendly." He drew her just a little closer as he remembered his cousin's flirtatious bent. "Perhaps too friendly."

"Darcy, I am happy to have found you," Rycroft said as he swung down from his horse. "My mother told me about your betrothal, and I wished to congratulate you in person."

Darcy raised a brow in question. "You have come from town to congratulate me?"

"No, no," he said, tossing the reins for his horse to the groom who accompanied him. "I have not yet reached town. I was on my way there but decided to stop at Bingley's new place before continuing on to town." He bowed to Elizabeth. "You must be Miss Bennet."

"I am one Miss Bennet." She motioned to the others who had not yet joined them but were drawing near. "There are four others."

His eyes grew wide, and Darcy watched Elizabeth bite back a smile at his cousin's shocked expression. "Five Miss Bennets?"

"Indeed," said Darcy. "The one on Bingley's arm is Miss Jane Bennet, the eldest. Next, there is Miss Elizabeth, my betrothed. And then Miss Mary, Miss Kitty, and Miss Lydia. In that order."

"Which is which?" Rycroft asked.

"Mary has flowers on her bonnet and is walking by herself, while Kitty and Lydia both favour ribbons on their bonnets. Lydia is the one who is talking," Elizabeth explained. "We are only walking a bit farther before returning to the house. Would you care to join us, my lord?"

"Mr. Bennet is ill," Darcy inserted before Rycroft could accept Elizabeth's invitation. He was unsure if he wished to have another member of his family impose upon the Bennet home while Mr. Bennet was still so unwell. He was also not particularly fond of the idea of his cousin, who was known for his charm, spending time with Elizabeth's sisters, though he was certain Miss Lydia would enjoy it.

"Is Bingley staying for a visit?" Rycroft asked. "I only ask because I stopped at Netherfield before coming here. It is only his sisters and Hurst who are there, and I did not wish to spend my time with his sisters."

Again, Darcy saw Elizabeth bite back a smile as she saw the look on Lord Rycroft's face, for he looked as if he had bitten an apple that was not quite ripe. To Darcy, it was a fitting expression of how unpleasant being fawned over by Miss Bingley could be.

"He is, but..." He let the rest of his thought hang in the air. He was certain his cousin knew what the rest would be by the smile the curled his lips and the laughter that danced in his eyes.

"Do not worry, Darcy," Rycroft said, proving that he did indeed understand what Darcy had not said. "Your lovely lady is safe from my charms. I shall be pleasant and civil, but I shall refrain from being my devilishly charming self in her presence." He winked at Elizabeth.

"And her sisters?" Darcy's tone held a warning that his cousin would not and did not miss.

"Two seem quite young," he said, "and one is smitten by Bingley, but there is the middle sister..." he added in a teasing tone.

He held up his hands when Darcy glared at him. "I jest. She is much too studious in appearance to be of interest to me. Much too serious."

Darcy saw Miss Mary stop and look in their direction before walking away quickly. Elizabeth must have seen it too, for she looked at him with a pained expression and said, "I am not sure what the issue is with the gentlemen in your family, Mr. Darcy, but it seems they have a propensity for insulting the ladies in mine."

Lord Rycroft looked first at Elizabeth and then at Miss Mary. "It was a jest!" He cried, clearly dismayed by what had just transpired. "Darcy knows how I have been teased all my life because I am not as quick at learning as he is. I promise you that it was not a disparagement of your sister."

"You may wish to explain that to her," Elizabeth said. "However, she may not be easily convinced of your innocence for she has always been teased about being too studious." She excused herself from them and hurried toward Mary.

Rycroft removed his hat and ran his hand through his hair. "I have not had a formal introduction, or I would run after her and explain."

And Darcy knew he would. Rycroft was not one to allow misunderstandings to fester if he was the cause of them.

"If I could give you some advice." Darcy placed an arm around his cousin's shoulders. "Your charm will not work on Miss Mary like it would on many of the ladies in town. Miss Mary is serious and sensible, Georgiana's friend, and a favourite of your mother."

Rycroft groaned, and Darcy knew he was likely imagining his poorly chosen words being repeated to Lady Sophia. "Miss Mary has met my mother?"

Darcy nodded and removed his arm from his cousin's shoulders. "Both she and Miss Elizabeth have. They accompanied me to London for a week before their father fell ill and they were called home."

"Is he gravely ill?"

"He is improving, but yes. He has made his last wishes known to me."

Rycroft blew out a breath. "Perhaps I should take my chances with Bingley's sisters."

"No," Darcy said, "an angry Miss Bennet is still better company than a happy Miss Bingley."

Rycroft laughed loudly at the comment, causing all to stop and look at him.

"Come," Darcy said. "I will introduce you to my new family. But please, try to make a better impression than Lady Catherine did earlier today."

"Aunt Catherine was here?"

"She was."

"I suppose she is displeased that you are not marrying Anne?"

"You could say that."

Darcy watched Elizabeth link arms with Mary and hand her a handkerchief. It was not a good start to his cousin's visit.

"Allow me to tell you about our aunt's visit."

And he did.

He related to his cousin the full content of the conversation in the Bennets' sitting room and then proceeded to tell him about the opinion of Lord

Matlock to his betrothal, as well as his reply to his uncle. Although his cousin joked about being the lesser intelligent man of the two of them, Darcy knew that he was anything but unintelligent and would hear the caution in the tale. Elizabeth and, by extension, her family were of great importance to him, and any disparagement would not be tolerated.

Rycroft nodded and clapped Darcy on the shoulder. "Point taken, Darcy. I shall be on my best behaviour. I promise."

# Chapter 18

The next week passed with all the flitting and fluttering one would expect when a wedding breakfast worthy of a man of Darcy's consequence was being planned by a woman such as Mrs. Bennet. Elizabeth escaped from her mother as often as she could to walk with Mr. Darcy or to sit with her father, who steadily improved. Still, by the morning of her wedding, she was quite ready for the ordeal to be done.

The service, on the morning of the delightful day when Elizabeth Bennet took on the new name of Mrs. Darcy, was solemn and sweet as is proper and expected. Her father had insisted upon attending her to the church and doing his part. He valiantly tried to refrain from tears but had on one occasion found it necessary to cough into his handkerchief in such a way as to catch an errant tear.

Now, with the ceremony behind them, Darcy guided Elizabeth down the hall and away from the throngs of people gathered in Netherfield's ballroom, which had been decorated to host the wedding breakfast. Mrs. Bennet would not hear of not having a wedding breakfast when Elizabeth had insisted that the preparations would be too much for her father and that she would be satisfied to have just a small family gathering. Mr. Bingley had stepped into the breach and proposed a compromise when the discussion had entered its second half-hour. And so, Netherfield's ballroom was now filled with family and friends eager to celebrate the union of Darcy and Elizabeth while the happy couple sought a few moments of solace in the place where they tended to find such relief from the busyness of a soiree.

There's was not to be an easy escape, however.

"Darcy," Lord Matlock said, impeding their progress down the hall outside of the ballroom.

"'My lord, I had not expected you to journey to Hertfordshire for my wedding breakfast." He tucked Elizabeth's arm close to his side and covered her hand with his. She understood his actions as those meant to protect her, and she loved him for it. Lord Matlock had declined Mr. Darcy's invitation to meet her, and she knew that he was one of her new husband's most contrary relations.

"I would not have — it is not customary, you know. However, my sister insisted on putting forth a show of support. She said something about a unified family having a stronger position in the *ton*." He took a sip of his drink and gave it a questioning look.

Apparently, the beverage was not up to his standards, though it was, according to Uncle Gardiner, some of the best that could be had.

"Not at all like the way things are done in true society," he muttered before cocking his head to the side and examining Elizabeth. One brow was raised slightly, and his lips formed a bit of a scowl. "So, you are Miss Bennet?"

She glanced briefly at Darcy with an amused look on her face. She wanted for no one's approval other than that of the handsome man holding her close to her side. She would not allow his uncle – her new uncle – no matter his station, to intimidate her or cause her to feel less than she was.

"I am sorry, but I am not." She saw her husband's lips twitch in amusement before she turned her attention back to Lord Matlock, whose brow was furrowed and whose scowl had deepened.

"You are not?" His tone was filled with ridicule.

"No, my lord, I am not. I cannot rightly say how things are done in *true* society, but in *this* society, when a lady joins her hand with a gentleman in marriage, she leaves her name behind and takes his. So, although, I was Miss Bennet earlier this morning, I am no longer she. I believe I am now Mrs. Darcy."

His eyes narrowed slightly. "You are very impertinent," he said.

"So I have been told, my lord, but I assure you that I am only so when the offending party has fired the first shot, as it were."

"Offending party!" he sputtered.

Elizabeth smiled at him. "Yes, my lord. I have not yet had a formal introduction to you, and you have already told me that you are here against your wishes and that the proceedings which have been carefully arranged to my preference and that of Mr. Darcy do not meet your standard for true society. Thus," she held up a finger as he opened his mouth to speak, "indicating that you feel all in attendance, including myself and my husband, to be beneath your notice. These things are considered offensive in *this* society."

Lady Sophia, who had come to stand behind her brother, chuckled softly. "Well-spoken, Mrs. Darcy." She lifted her glass in salute. "Darcy, have you not introduced your wife to your uncle?"

"I have not had the opportunity, Aunt Sophia."

Lady Sophia stepped forward and gave first Elizabeth a kiss and then Darcy. "You look lovely, Mrs. Darcy, and contrary to the opinion of some, I find the breakfast to be well-done. I know a few in my acquaintance who would be green with envy to see how excellent everything is."

She stepped back and motioned for Darcy to do his duty in making introductions, which he did.

Although Lord Matlock only deigned to give a small bow and mumble a word of greeting, Elizabeth performed a proper curtsey and assured him of the pleasure it was to meet him. Her behavior would be above reproach even if his was lacking.

Lady Sophia winked at Darcy. "I believe you were whisking your lady away somewhere when my brother stopped you, were you not?"

Darcy's ears felt warm. He had hoped to sneak Elizabeth away without being noticed. "I was," he said. "I had a gift for my bride that I wished for her to have during the breakfast."

"Well," his aunt said as she slipped her arm through her brother's, "do not let us detain you." She pulled her brother toward the ballroom. "Come, and do try to be civilized and polite."

"Civilized?" Lord Matlock sputtered. "Of all the impertinent things! I am always civilized."

"While that may be true," Lady Sophia said, "you are not always polite." And then, she continued to scold him as they walked down the hall.

Elizabeth giggled softly behind her hand. "She is very bold."

"She is much like you." Darcy drew her down the hall toward the library once again. "Just like you she is a beautiful woman with a strong mind..."

"And an impertinent nature?" she asked as he closed the door behind them.

He nodded. "I have always liked that about my aunt, and while I am not as fond of the trait in my sister, I find it beguiling in you." He pulled her to him and kissed her softly. Then, he took her hand and led her to the chair she had been sitting in on the night of the Netherfield ball – that fateful night which had brought about this wonderful day.

"As I said, I have a gift for you. One of many actually." He moved to the shelf that was home to works of poetry and retrieved the parcel he had stashed there this morning.

"Oh, I do like presents," she said excitedly, causing him to laugh. He loved her light and lively spirit.

"This is the first. Another awaits you in the carriage, and if my message was received and my directions followed, there are a few awaiting you when we get to London." He placed a small velvet bag in her hands.

He waited as patiently as he was able while she untied the ribbon that held the bag closed and then widened the opening so she could retrieve his gift.

"Oh, these are lovely," she exclaimed as she drew out two lavender shoe roses that had a few clear glass beads sewn to the edges of the petals.

"I asked Mary to assist me with making sure they would attach properly to the buttons on your shoes today." He knelt at her feet. "May I?"

She lifted the edge of her skirt and allowed him

to replace the roses on her slippers. "Do you always remove your slippers when reading?" he asked.

She laughed. "Not always, but nearly so."

"I remember seeing your slippers under your chair a few times when you were reading during your sister's illness." He leaned back on his heels and admired the roses. They suited her. "I dare say your father is aware of your habit, is he not?"

She nodded. "I am sure he is as he has tripped over my slippers in his study more than once." She gasped as what Darcy was hinting at bloomed into understanding in her mind.

"He knew that my aunt would see me without slippers and would embellish the tale of us being alone. Oh, he is most devious!"

While her words were those which might be uttered harshly, they were not spoken with anything more than a hint of laughter. There was no longer any doubt in Darcy's mind that she was happy with how the events in the library that night had turned out – not that the process to get here had been utterly enjoyable. He could still remember her tears as she cried at the thought of being forced to marry him. However, her smile as she twisted her foot one way and then another admiring how the beads sparkled in the light was the memory which he would tuck away in his heart and recall whenever he entered a library, whether here at Netherfield or elsewhere. Elizabeth was his, and she was happy to be so.

"They are beautiful." Her eyes lifted from her toes to him.

"Nearly as beautiful as the lady who wears them." He took her hands and drew from her chair. "We must return before we are missed. I would not wish your aunt to have more stories to share about us."

She giggled as he pulled her into his arms.

"Let them talk. For what can they say that is not true? I love my husband and libraries."

"And I love my wife," he replied before placing a kiss on her lips and exiting the library.

# Chapter 19

"Oh, Lizzy!" Mrs. Bennet took her by the arm as she and Darcy entered the room. "Mrs. Long has been looking for you to congratulate you as has been Lady Lucas."

Elizabeth gave her mother a skeptical look. "They have been looking, or you have been looking so that you can remind them of your good fortune?"

Mrs. Bennet chuckled. "Well, I dare say I have reason to do so. They have forever been saying how much trouble I would have marrying off five daughters. Be that as it may, I have one who is married and another who is well on her way, for we know Mr. Bingley will not be able to resist Jane's charms forever. Indeed, he has already made his intentions known by courting her."

She paused to look around the room. "Oh, there

they are." She pulled Elizabeth toward a group of ladies who were chattering in the corner. "You know neither Mrs. Long nor Lady Lucas has a daughter attached to any gentleman. One married and another as good as, and they each only have one daughter and still have not done so well as I."

Elizabeth fought the urge to roll her eyes.

"It was clever of me to have Jane become ill. I dare say, your time at Netherfield is when Mr. Darcy began to change his mind about you."

Elizabeth shared a look with Darcy, who only shrugged and smiled.

"Yes, yes," she continued to herself, "that must be it, for when else would he have come to know you well enough." She drew Darcy and Elizabeth into the circle of ladies and preened as the ladies gave their congratulations and wishes for health and joy.

As they left the group of ladies, Darcy leaned close to Elizabeth's ear. "One hour, my love, and then we shall need to leave if we wish to reach town in time for Mrs. Vernon's dinner."

"Mrs. Bennet," Lady Sophia said as she took Mrs. Bennet's arm. "This is a fine fete. One of the best I have attended, and I am not given to meaningless flattery."

Together, the two ladies walked toward the far end of the room where the piano had been placed. Georgiana and Mary were seated comfortably at it, taking turns playing.

"My niece will no doubt be returning to her brother's home as soon as he and Mrs. Darcy are settled, and I shall be quite alone."

"But do you not have a son?" Mrs. Bennet asked.

"I do." A son she would like to see married. "However, he is often gone to our estate, and when he is in town, he has his friends and clubs. He is not inattentive, mind you, but he is not the sort to sit and stitch with his mother."

"I would be surprised if any gentleman were the sort to do so," Mrs. Bennet's voice was filled with surprise.

"Precisely," Lady Sophia agreed as she watched Mary turn the pages for Georgiana. Theirs was a friendship she was glad to see and wished to nurture for the sake of both young ladies. With that in mind, she turned her attention back to Mrs. Bennet.

"I was wondering if I could be so bold as to ask

that you allow me the company of one of your daughters. I have the means by which to sponsor a young lady for a season, and Miss Mary is such a delight."

"Mary?" Mrs. Bennet looked at Mary as if never having seen the girl before. "Mary is a delight?"

"Indeed, I find her so, but I am not typical."

"You would like to give my Mary a season in town?" The excitement was building in Mrs. Bennet's voice.

"Yes, Mrs. Bennet, I would, and as a countess and the mother of the Earl Rycroft, I can guarantee she would be given the greatest opportunities to meet and mingle with many eligible young gentlemen." She smiled and whispered, "You may find yourself with three married daughters before any of the others have even one. Although I cannot guarantee it will happen," at least not with great certainty, "I do think with a bit of specific training — which I can arrange — she will take quite well. You may even find she has more than one offer from a worthy gentleman."

"Oh, my lady, you do us a great honor. I would be delighted to allow Mary to stay with you for the season." Mrs. Bennet's fan fluttered with the excitement of it all.

"And I am elated to know I shall have such excellent company."

Mary had not meant to be listening, but, being close to where her mother and Lady Sophia were talking, she had heard the majority of the conversation. She was to go to town for the season?

"Oh, Mary," Georgiana whispered, "I shall be so glad to have you near. Is it not exciting?"

Mary nodded. A sense of freedom welled within her.

"Of what are we conversing about in whispers, dear cousin?" Lord Rycroft drew a chair near them.

Mary lifted a brow in disapproval. "It is not polite to ask about another's private conversations."

"I do apologize, Miss Mary, but you both looked so delighted, I found myself overcome by curiosity." It was not the first apology he had offered her, and he suspected it would not be the last. He had offended her, and true to what Darcy had said, a Bennet lady did not forgive an offense readily. She had said she accepted the apology, but her manners still said otherwise.

"Would it be impolite of me to request that you play that last song once again? I rather enjoyed it."

She gave him a wary look. "Some might find it repetitive to listen to the same piece twice in a row." She took her music from the instrument. "I shall play it, but not until after I have had a moment to walk around and partake of a glass of punch." She rose and dipped a quick curtsey. "If you will excuse me."

"Did you offend her?" Georgiana asked, turning toward her cousin.

"Why do you ask?" He said, stretching his legs out in front of him.

"Because she was rather cross." Georgiana crossed her arms and scowled at him.

"I may have said something as a jest that she found offensive, but I have apologized. She is just unwilling to forgive."

"Hmph," huffed Georgiana. She spread her music out on the piano and began to play. "Since you have driven her away, you will need to pay attention so that you can turn the pages for me."

~*~

Darcy watched Mary cross the room. "I see your sister is still not on friendly terms with Rycroft."

Elizabeth laughed lightly. "She is not." She leaned a bit closer to Darcy. "She says he smiles too much to be trustworthy."

Darcy chuckled. "He seems intent upon having her forgive him. I have not seen him so persistent in trying to obtain a pardon from anyone — gentleman or lady. Of course, he has not offended a family member in some time, and she is now family."

"Very true," Elizabeth agreed. "She will forgive him in time...probably, but then again, how much will she be in company with him? It is not like he will have reason to travel to Hertfordshire, and Papa does not go to town."

"She will visit us, and it is likely he will visit as well. There shall be times when they will be in company," Darcy said. "Rycroft does not visit so often as Richard, but he is not an unfamiliar guest in my study."

Elizabeth sighed. "In that case, we shall just have to hope all is well by then."

~*~

"Bennet." Sir William handed his friend a cup of tea and joined him in sitting in a small alcove that afforded him a view of the room but kept him removed from any draft.

Mr. Bennet had had a difficult time convincing any of his family to allow him to journey to Netherfield to observe the festivities. But this was not a day he would miss.

"They appear happy, and it has happened before they were married," Sir William said.

"They are happy. I have spent many hours in bed watching them as they sat with me." Mr. Bennet smiled and sipped the warm tea. He watched Darcy talking to Elizabeth, and then as something had obviously concerned her, for she had sighed, he had watched Darcy wink at her and lift her hand to his lips. "It is a very good match."

"And Jane's happiness is also nearly secured." Sir William nodded to where Bingley and Jane stood quietly conversing together.

"And Collins is gone." Mr. Bennet sighed. "But he shall return. He insists on mending fences, which is something that cannot be done without the entail being broken, but he does not see that." They sat in silence for some minutes, each drinking their tea.

"I have heard from my wife that you are planning a journey to the seaside after the winter," commented Sir William.

Mr. Bennet nodded. "If I tarry." He pulled in a less shallow breath. "I do wish to see all my daughters so happy as Lizzy, but I fear my heart may expire before then."

Sir William gave him a sympathetic smile. "Well, then, Mary is next. Who shall we select for her?" He rubbed his hands together.

Mr. Bennet chuckled softly. "I shall not be selecting any other husbands, but, do not fear, Mary's future is well in hand." He nodded to where his wife stood with Lady Sophia. "I believe she will be having a season if Darcy's aunt has her way. It seems the lady has taken a liking to my Mary."

"She is a sweet girl."

"That she is. A bit fond of sermons, but sweet and good. I have no doubt she will shine away from her sisters."

"Papa." Elizabeth did not wish to interrupt her father's conversation, but it was time to take her leave and the longer she waited, the more difficult the idea was becoming.

"Ah, my Lizzy, is it time?" He looked to Darcy, who was standing behind Elizabeth.

"I am afraid it is, sir."

"Very good," Mr. Bennet said as he began to push up from his chair.

"No, Papa."

"I shall stand and give my daughter a hug and see her to the door." He stood slowly. Sir William stood at his elbow ready to assist him if he should need it. "Come, give me a hug and make it a good one as it shall have to serve me well until the spring."

"I love you, Papa," Elizabeth whispered as she squeezed him tightly.

"And I, you, my dear Lizzy." He kissed her cheek and then placed her hand in Darcy's. "I know you will care for her well."

"I will, sir. Thank you." Darcy took Elizabeth's hand, tucked in the crook of his elbow, and held it there.

Mr. Bennet took up his walking stick and placed a hand on his friend's arm. "I shall follow you to the door, Lizzy, but it may take me a while. I do not move so quickly as I once did." He coughed lightly into his handkerchief.

Darcy walked slowly toward the door with Elizabeth on his arm. A few from the room had moved into the hall to farewell the newlyweds, but all stood to the side and allowed Mr. Bennet to pass. Jane and Bingley stood at the door with Mrs. Bennet. Elizabeth paused to give her mother and sister a hug, and then waited for her father to reach the door, so that she could give him one more brief hug before descending the stairs to the waiting carriage. She turned as she entered it and gave a final wave to those who were waiting.

"Are you well, my love?" Darcy asked as he took his seat next to her and wrapped his arms around her.

"I am." She snuggled into his embrace. "He chose well." She smiled up at him.

"He did indeed." He stroked her cheek and brushed a thumb across her lips before bending to kiss them. She sighed and pressed her lips more firmly against his as she had done the first time he kissed her.

He had intended to give her the book he had requested from Bingley — the one she had been reading when the compromise had occurred — and perhaps he would give it to her in a while. But for now, he was content to revel in the privilege of holding her and kissing her as no other man had.

And as her hands slid up his chest and around

his neck, he said a word of thanks for having been fortunate enough to be her father's choice.

# Before You Go

If you enjoyed this book, be sure to let others know by leaving a review.

~*~*~

Want to know when other Leenie books will be available?
You can always know what's new with my books by subscribing to my mailing list.
(There will, of course, be a thank you gift for joining because I think my readers are awesome!)
Book News from Leenie Brown
(bit.ly/LeenieBBookNews)

~*~*~

Turn the page to read an excerpt from *No Other Choice*, the next book in the Choices series.

# No Other Choice
## Excerpt

## DECEMBER 18, 1811

Lord Samuel Rycroft blinked and looked at his mother as if he was unable to understand what she had said. He took off his hat and placed it on the table in the entryway at Netherfield. "Pardon me?"

"I said we will depart for town when Miss Mary arrives." His mother made her way back into the sitting room and peered out the window. "There is no need to fear. She knows I am always early."

"I am still not understanding why we must wait for Miss Mary." He unbuttoned his greatcoat and began to shrug out of it. He had hoped to be in the carriage by now and on his way to town.

"Good morning, Georgiana," said Lady Sophia. "Did you have something to eat, my dear?"

"Yes, thank you." Georgiana laid her outerwear on the settee with her aunt's things and took a seat near the window, so that she could see the drive. "I cannot wait for Miss Mary to arrive. It will be ever so pleasant to have her company."

"Company?" Rycroft's brows drew together. "Surely, we must not wait for you to finish a visit before leaving." He had things to do in town and a sister of Bingley's to avoid. He definitely did not have time for a social call.

Georgiana laughed. "A visit? At this time of the morning? I think not, Cousin. Miss Mary is to travel with us."

Lady Sophia sighed at her son's still puzzled expression. "She is coming to stay with me. Georgiana will soon be able to return to her brother, and I do not wish to be lonely." She smoothed her skirt over her legs. With her eyes lowered as they were she could not see his expression, which was her intent, but she could see his toe start to tap as the silence in the room grew. She looked up at him with a smile and then turned to look out the window.

"A project, Mother?" It was not unlike his

mother to take on a less fortunate lady and help her to find a husband.

"No, no." She shook her head. "Miss Mary is not a project. She is a friend." She turned back to look at him. "I do like to have company of the female sort, and if that company happens to be a young lady of marriageable age and in need of some assistance, it makes me feel useful. It has been all arranged. Miss Mary will travel with us today and stay the week. We will visit the shops and arrange for her orders; then, she will return to Longbourn with her aunt and uncle for Christmas. She will rejoin us in the new year to participate in the season."

"A project." He ran his hands through his hair and shook his head. "And I am supposed to pay for this project?"

Lady Sophia crossed her arms. "Miss Mary is not a project. She is a friend and a guest of mine."

"Aunt," said Georgiana softly.

Rycroft sighed. "But you shall require me to attend all of the functions you select?"

"Well," said Lady Sophia, ignoring Georgiana's second soft call, "we shall need an escort, and you need to attend anyway if we ever expect to find you a wife."

"We do not need to find me a wife. I can do that on my own." He hated being reminded of his duty to the title and his need to marry. He had been looking, but there were not any young ladies who interested him. They were all so agreeable, so biddable, so boring.

"You have done a poor job of it thus far, my son." Lady Sophia cocked her head to the side and gave him a stern look. "If you will remember, I gave you until this season to sort it out for yourself. Now, I will assist you. The deadline has passed for you to continue on without my interference."

"Fine." His eyes narrowed and his jaw clenched slightly. "I shall trot about with you and your project, Miss Mary, but I shall make my own decision." He stiffened as he heard a gasp from the doorway behind him...

# Acknowledgements

There are many who have had a part in the creation of this story. Some have read and commented on it. Some have proofread for grammatical errors and plot holes. Others have not even read the story (and a few, I know, will never read it), but their encouragement and belief in my ability, as well as their patience when I became cranky or when supper was late or the groceries ran low, was invaluable.

And so, I would like to say *thank you* to Zoe, Rose, Betty, Kristine, Ben, and Kyle, as well as my faithful readers on my blog and at darcyandlizzy.com.

I have not listed my dear husband in that group because to me he deserves his own special thank you, for without his somewhat pushy insistence just over a year ago that I begin sharing my writing, none of my writing goals and dreams would have been met.

# Other Leenie B Books

You can find all of Leenie's books at this link
bit.ly/LeenieBBooks
where you can explore the collections below

~*~

Dash of Darcy and Companions Collection

~*~

Marrying Elizabeth Series

~*~

Willow Hall Romances

~*~

The Choices Series

~*~

Darcy Family Holidays

~*~

Darcy and... An Austen-Inspired Collection

~*~

Other Pens

~*~

Touches of Austen Collection

~*~

Nature's Fury and Delights

~*~

Teatime Tales

# About the Author

Leenie Brown has always been a girl with an active imagination, which, while growing up, was both an asset, providing many hours of fun as she played out stories, and a liability, when her older sister and aunt would tell her frightening tales. At one time, they had her convinced Dracula lived in the trunk at the end of the bed she slept in when visiting her grandparents!

Although it has been years since she cowered in her bed in her grandparents' basement, she still has an imagination which occasionally runs away with her, and she feeds it now as she did then — by reading!

Her heroes, when growing up, were authors, and the worlds they painted with words were (and still are) her favourite playgrounds! Now, as an adult, she spends much of her time in the Regency world, playing with the characters from her favourite Jane Austen novels and those of her own creation.

When she is not traipsing down a trail in an attempt to keep up with her imagination, Leenie resides in the beautiful province of Nova Scotia with her two sons and her very own Mr. Brown (a wonderful mix of all the best of Darcy, Bingley, and Edmund with a healthy dose of the teasing Mr. Tilney and just a dash of the scolding Mr. Knightley).

# Connect with Leenie

*E-mail:*
*LeenieBrownAuthor@gmail.com*
*Facebook:*
www.facebook.com/LeenieBrownAuthor
*Blog:*
*leeniebrown.com*
*Patreon:*
https://www.patreon.com/LeenieBrown
*Subscribe to Leenie's Mailing List:*
Book News from Leenie Brown
(bit.ly/LeenieBBookNews)